REESE KNIGHTLEY

CUTTING IT CLOSE

Infinity—A top secret US Army Special Forces unit that provides help, domestic and foreign, and answers only to the Secretary of Defense.

CUTTING IT CLOSE

CHAPTER ONE

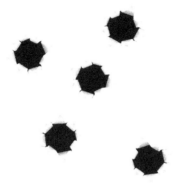

Maddox

I f Maddox Stone could have walked away and given it all up in that very moment, he would have. But that wasn't a luxury he could afford.

He drew a deep breath and let it out hard before he spoke between his teeth.

"I don't give a damn why you did it, you should have asked me first." He scowled at his business partner.

Bull Seeger frowned back. "I own half this ranch!"

He gave the man a narrowed look. "This ranch wouldn't even be solvent if it weren't for my grandfather."

"Well, thanks for that." Bull's face filled with hurt.

Not wanting to be pulled into Bull's manipulation, he steeled himself against the hurt in the old man's eyes. If he didn't get a handle on Bull's erratic spending, the guy was going to be out of a home.

"The truth hurts."

"You know what, Maddox? You can go to hell," Bull said and stomped slowly into the living room. The cane held tightly by a gnarled hand thumped on the floor.

With an overly long sigh, he stalked after the cranky old coot. "Look. I really don't have time to be running back here every time Triton calls me because you have some half-cocked scheme up your sleeve."

Bull lowered slowly to the sofa. "Yes. You're very busy." The man turned his face away and stared out the wide window that graced one half of the room.

"I am very busy!" He clenched his teeth. "I can't get back here more than once a year, you know that. I'll stay until I have this mess sorted out and then I'm gone."

"Don't put yourself out," Bull muttered. "I can handle it."

"Yeah, I see the way you handled it. We'll be lucky if we pull out of this one." He threw up his hands.

Bull flinched but didn't say another word.

The one thing Maddox had done through the years was support this place. Yet, every time he turned around, he got a call about money problems. Frankly, he was sick of it. With the next few days free, he could look into the problem, but he didn't always have free time. He was a very busy man. More so than Bull realized.

Striding into the kitchen, his spurs rang on the hardwood floor as he strode past the kitchen table to the back door.

"Jim," he snapped at the ranch foreman just lifting a forkful of eggs to his mouth. Jim Lancaster had been the Triple R foreman since before his grandfather bought into the ranch. Jim shoved back his chair, the half-eaten food pushed aside.

"Yes sir?"

"I'm headed to the east barn," he growled on his way out the back door.

The man gulped, grabbed the toast from his plate, his coat from the hook near the door, and followed after him.

Stalking to the main horse barn, he looked over the state of the ranch. As things went, it wasn't in too bad of shape physically. The landscape around the main house looked good and the structure of the buildings looked sound. The livestock were healthy.

What wasn't good was the financial aspects of running the place. Every time he turned around, he was having to sink his hard earned money into the place.

"You know…" Jim said, running after him. The older man huffed and puffed a bit when he caught up. "Bull is getting on in years."

He ignored Jim and yanked open the east barn door and stepped inside.

"He didn't mean no harm."

"You'd do well to spend more time doing your job than defending Bull's actions," he clipped out.

Jim twisted his cap and nodded before turning away.

He closed his eyes, spun around, and stalked down the long length to the end of the barn.

Toward the rear door, the mare in the foaling stall stomped and pulled at the lead rope one of the ranch hands was holding.

"Fucking hold still!" The guy smacked the mare on the muzzle and she cried out in distress.

In two large strides, he fisted the back of the man's shirt. His other hand came around and clamped on the pressure point on the man's wrist. The guy yelled and dropped the lead rope. Spinning the man around, Maddox punched him in the nose before shoving him to the dirt.

"What!" The guy scrambled back on his ass, hands holding his nose.

Maddox towered over the guy. "Collect your check."

"Wait. She's -"

"She's in pain. I won't say it again. Collect your check and get off my land," he snarled, taking a step forward.

Scrambling, the man jumped to his feet and ran.

He spun and eased up to the skittish mare in the stall.

"Whoa…" He caught the lead rope, careful to leave slack, and lifted a hand to smooth over the red gleaming coat of the skittish mare. She jerked beneath his touch.

"He had that coming," his young cousin said from behind him.

Ignoring Triton, he ran his gaze over the mare. His mouth grew tight. She was only hours from giving birth. "Easy, girl, you're going to be fine, you can do this," he coaxed.

"You talk to her like she's human," Triton said, moving closer, almost to his shoulder.

Maddox sent his cousin a look and caught the quick flashing smile. His cousin was always smiling. People liked the young man and gravitated toward his happy disposition.

"She's more human than some people I know," he growled.

Triton snorted. The twenty-one year old was cute; all brown curly hair, big, bright eyes, slim, and stood around five feet eleven inches. Not as tall as he or bulky, but not everyone could be as big as him. There was a twelve year age gap between him and his younger cousin, but that never mattered to them. Triton, kicked out of his aunt and uncle's house because he'd come out as gay, had moved to the ranch three years ago to live and go to college. Maddox had welcomed Triton with open arms and they'd grown close. When he was on leave, Maddox came home in the summer, teaching Triton the ropes of the ranch. The young man had taken to ranching like a duck to water.

"I heard you and Bull fighting earlier," Triton said.

He gave a hard sigh.

"He did fuck up the finances again, didn't he?" Triton asked, and then shook his head.

His cousin had been the one to leave the message at the base, the message that had brought him home. Maddox had called home and caught a flight out the very next day. Luckily, Major Jones had granted his military leave. But that was only because the target of their next assignment had gone dark before they could deploy, leaving Maddox with enough time to deal with this bullshit.

"Bull took out a loan against the ranch to expand barn number three, so he could rent out the inside for storage." Maddox removed the mare's halter. Sliding it off her muzzle, he hung it near the stall.

"I saw the expansion. I wondered where he got the money. For a minute, I thought you okayed it. I didn't know any different until you called me."

"No, I wouldn't have okayed something like that!" he snapped. "We had only enough to make it through this coming winter without adding a loan payment to the bills. He's cut the ranch short. And I haven't seen one payment coming in from the rental. That type of expansion needs to be planned for. And that's why Tanner's Feed Store called you about their unpaid bill."

"Bull's been having the hands buy cheaper feed over at Smith's."

A slow throbbing began behind his temple and he lifted a hand to rub at the spot.

"Bull took money out of the ranch account. A lot of it. I don't know where it is." It pissed him off and worried him. When he was pissed, he lost his temper, and when he lost his temper…well, the results weren't pretty.

"Anything I can do to help? I can skip a few classes."

"Keep your ass in college," he snapped.

"Cuz. What the hell?" Triton said incredulously.

"You asked." He squinted at his cousin.

"You don't need to be an asshole to me." Triton threw up his hands. "I didn't borrow money against the ranch. Or wipe the account out. Don't take it out on me!"

Maddox made a sound in the back of his throat.

"I wish River was here!" Triton said with a glare.

"You didn't even know him!" he shouted, and the mare stomped away from him. He shut the birthing stall and stalked to the end of the barn.

"Mad!" Triton called from behind him.

He stopped in the open doorway.

"I'm sorry," Triton said, drawing close. "I shouldn't have said that. You're right, I don't know him."

"Then why'd you say it?"

"Because Bull said you never used to yell when River was around."

"Well, that was a long time ago," he muttered. A life-time ago since it had all fallen apart and he wished for nothing more than to step back in time and make it right. But he couldn't. "And I have bigger shit to deal with. So either help me or take off," he said through clenched teeth, angry as all hell.

Triton didn't leave, he just stood quietly next to him.

"Think it'll rain?" Triton wisely changed the subject.

"Nah, but you know what they say, give it fifteen minutes." He took a long, slow breath and readjusted his hat before he tugged the brim down low and moved outside of the wide open doors of the barn. Triton followed and they stood together looking over his legacy. A lump grew in his throat and he rubbed a hand over his mouth. It was the only thing he had left of his grandfather, Andrew Stone.

It was also the only thing left to remind him of his mistakes. Mistakes that had come at a price. He still came home every summer, waiting and hoping for the chance to make it right. He didn't think anything could do that and regret formed a knot in his gut.

What he needed to do now was keep Bull from running the ranch into the ground. His cousin was turning out to be a big help and when he left his part of the ranch to someone, he'd pick Triton.

Someday, this would all belong to Triton and River.

"How long are you staying?" Triton gazed up at him.

"Not long," he rasped, and even though he'd been an asshole, the young man's face fell. He couldn't stay long. He had a mission to get back to.

"Have you been staying out here instead of the dorms?" he asked Triton.

"When I can, I do. I like helping with the horses, and the college campus is not far."

Triton's phone buzzed. His cousin made a face.

"Who's that?"

"Clay, he wants me to pick up some dinner on the way back to town."

"You don't want to go?"

"Not really." Triton shrugged.

"Problems?" He leaned a shoulder against the barn door.

"Just need some time alone." Triton flashed him a quick smile, moving to stand beside him.

"Make sure he's what you want," Maddox said of his cousin's boyfriend.

His cousin smiled and elbowed him. "I know, I know!"

Maddox grabbed Triton by the head and gave him a knuckle rub and then jumped back. He didn't play around often, so he took Triton completely by surprise. So much so, the kid stood with his mouth gaping.

He jogged back into the barn in the direction of the foaling mare. Beyond her stall, the far barn door stood open allowing the small breeze to blow through the building. From there, he could see the other row of massive barns.

"The number three barn door is open." He frowned at the newly renovated metal of the barn Bull had spent the damn money on.

"Yeah, it's that monthly rental thing. I saw them pull up as I was coming to find you."

"The big rig?"

"Yeah."

"They're tearing up the grass." He frowned at the deep tire marks in the green that separated each barn.

"I'll go see about the open door and tell them to be

careful," Triton offered and took off out the back door toward the barn.

"Collect a payment if you can!" he called after his cousin. The young man gave a thumbs up before jogging away.

Once Maddox had the stall door reopened, he eased toward the mare. She danced away from him, and regret he'd frightened her tightened his mouth. It took him several long minutes to soothe and calm her down.

CHAPTER TWO

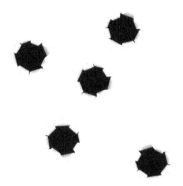

River

"ALPHA TEAM, WHAT IS YOUR POSITION?" INFINITY'S dispatcher asked through the mic.

First Lieutenant River Seeger pressed the small mic in his ear. "Alpha team, south rear entrance."

"Roger, Alpha team," dispatch responded, and then after a moment, added, "Bravo, Charlie teams, confirm positions, over."

"Charlie team, front entrance," Sergeant Diesel Gannon replied.

Easing upward a bit, River took in the small porch and the closed backdoor. The paint on both the porch and the door was cracked and cratered. The wood should easily give way. He slowly crouched back down.

"Easy peasy," Sergeant Isaac Thorne whispered and waggled his eyebrows through the eye slit in his mask. Then the soldier walked a knife through the fingers of one black gloved hand as casual as you fucking please.

Hunkered down next to them, Sergeant Blade Hammond rolled her eyes and gave Isaac a suffering look before she pulled down her face mask.

River pulled on his oxygen mask and the rest of the team followed suit.

From their left, Sergeant Ethan Caufield ran in a crouching run. When the man reached the house, he spider climbed up the side and crept across the roof.

"Attic entrance. Bravo out," Ethan finally replied through the mic once he reached the entry point from above.

"Roger that. Infinity, mission is a go," dispatch said.

Leaping to the porch, River kicked in the old door. Wood splintered with a loud crack.

River went in low with Isaac and Blade at his back. The house was small, maybe three bedrooms, and as a result, the floor shook when the rest of his unit slammed entry at once. It had the desired effect.

The windows blew in at the den. He ducked back for a moment. A loud crack from the flash grenade erupted and then he was moving around the corner and back into the room.

Drug addicts scattered, coughing and hacking in the smoke. Two long-haired, shirtless, skeletal-looking men flew from the hole-riddled couch. The glass from a mirror shattered and tumbled to the ground with a crash, razor blades flew, and white powder sprayed the air and the stained carpet. A lamp was kicked over in the fray. Three half-dressed women screamed and ran for various rooms.

One came right at him, and when she swung, he gripped her arms, twisted, and placed them behind her back before shoving her at Blade. In seconds, Blade zip-tied the woman's hands and shoved her toward the back door where more of their team waited.

River kept moving, gun raised, and with one hand cupping the other, he moved swiftly across the living room and down the hallway. He reached the last bedroom door, yanked off his mask, and waited until Isaac and Blade were at the other two bedroom doors. Ethan, having dropped down from the attic opening, stood in the middle of the hallway.

Giving a nod, River kicked in the bedroom door simultaneously as the other two kicked in the other bedroom doors. He went in at a roll as a shot was fired and punched through the wall above his head.

The obese gunman sat on the bed holding a young, terrified girl in front of him as a shield. She wasn't really big enough to cover much of the guy.

The man's gun was pointed at him. "Get back!"

River shot the guy in the leg and the man screamed and reached down, clutching his knee. River kept coming across the room, he had closed the distance before the guy could fucking blink.

Pressing the obese man's head down between his legs, River easily held the guy hunched over. Within a moment, he had completely disarmed him.

In the next instant, the tiny girl fell from the perp's grip and went scrambling up and running for the door.

"I've got her," Blade said, scooping up the crying child.

"Close the door on your way out," River told Blade quietly.

"Wait!" the man called out with a face turned red from being held hunched over.

The door closed and River put his boot to the guy's chest and shoved. The overly large man went toppling back onto the bed.

River field-stripped the suspect's gun while the perp rolled around and then finally managed to sit back up.

"What are you going to do?" Fear darkened the man's eyes.

"You like to hurt women and children. What do you think I *should* do?" River sneered, studying the man like a bug.

"You can't kill me."

"I can't?" He lifted his own gun and put it to the fucker's forehead.

Sweat trickled down the suspect's face.

"Where's Lieutenant Seeger?" Captain Elijah Cobalt's deep voice boomed through the house and bounced in his ear off the mic.

"He's in the back room with the child abuser, Captain," Isaac said like it was no big deal.

"Shit!"

The house jumped a bit when Elijah's big boots pounded on the wooden floor. A few seconds later, the door was thrown open and Elijah's large frame filled up the open doorway.

"You gotta help me!" the guy's voice wobbled.

"You good, Lieutenant?" Elijah drawled.

"Yup, I'm good, Captain."

Sweat rolled down the fucker's face.

After another long, tense moment, River sneered before shoving away. Lifting his gun from the man's forehead, he spun and gave Elijah a nod.

"He was gonna kill me!"

"Shut the fuck up or I will," Elijah snarled and hauled the hefty guy upward with one big, beefy hand.

Snatching his mask from the floor, River moved out into the hallway and headed toward the main room.

Isaac waited and offered him a cocky grin when he approached.

"Where's the girl?" he asked, ignoring his friend's questioning look.

"Soon to be on her way back to her mother," Isaac said.

"Unfortunately," he scowled.

He didn't envy the little girl and her mother, they had a long road ahead. He only hoped that the mother would finally leave the abusive bastard, but he wouldn't hold his breath. She'd gone back to the man three times and each time, she'd been abused worse than the last. This last time, she'd finally reported her husband and the man had fled across the border, taking their seven year old daughter with him. The little girl's mother was related to a United States senator, so Infinity had been called in to resolve the situation.

"What? Don't believe they can make it work?" Isaac eyed him.

"Good luck to that," he said coldly.

"Damn, River, bitter much?"

"I'm not bitter, I'm a realist," he said flatly, and Isaac snorted.

"Does your boyfriend know that?" the man grinned.

"Hey, Cris and I have level heads. We didn't become boyfriends lightly. We thought through things."

"Oh, that's right. No falling in love for you. What did

it take? Three years to even decide to call yourselves boyfriends?" Isaac laughed.

"That's not long." River frowned.

"Dude…" Isaac rolled his eyes. "Trust me. When it's the one, you don't wait three damned years to commit," Isaac said with a smirk.

River snapped his teeth and strode past Isaac and kept on walking into the small kitchen that led to the back door. He'd had that kind of instant love before but it didn't last. So what if he wasn't madly in love with Cris? River didn't believe in the whimsical nonsense of love.

"I'll be glad to see the last of this place," Isaac said, catching up with him.

River tucked his gun away, stepped outside into the warm Mexico weather, and took a deep breath to shake off the stench of the house.

Elijah came out of the house and strode toward him. River squinted at his captain, but the man said nothing other than look him over.

"Let's move it," Elijah said. River noticed the crowd gathering. They turned as one and jogged to the waiting Black Hawk, its rotary blades already spinning. The crowd threw bottles and garbage at them as the bird lifted off.

Snapping his seat belt, he sat across from the little girl. She gazed at him with wide eyes, a bruise standing out on one of her cheeks. So young, so innocent, she reminded him of a boy he'd known. Adults were supposed to protect children.

River clenched his teeth and tore his gaze away. Looking out over the landscape below, the little girl's abusive father was being handed over to the local authorities.

Good, the guy deserves to rot in a foreign prison. The patrol car was chased by the locals as it slowly drove away from the house.

The chopper dropped them off at a small, undisclosed airport a few miles over the U.S. border. The mother was there to collect her daughter, and she thanked them all profusely. The authorities would be looking at removing the child from the home unless the woman did something. He hoped to god she did.

From there, the unit boarded a small airplane that would take them back to headquarters. Infinity was temporarily housed in a top secret location bordering one of the west coast states. They were moved often. In fact, setting up a command center in the middle of nowhere wasn't unusual for them.

River was used to it, he'd been in Special Forces for almost eight years. Roughly five of those years had been with a top secret black ops unit called Infinity.

CHAPTER THREE

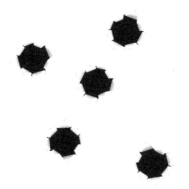

Maddox

"**B**oss?" Jim said from behind him.

"Yes?"

"I'm set to run out to the north pasture and bring in those heifers. You need me here for the mare?" the foreman asked.

"No. I can handle it." He glanced toward the door. "You better get going so you'll be back before dark."

"Will do."

"Jim?" he called before the older man could get to the end of the barn.

"Yes?"

"Sorry about before," he said gruffly when the man turned around.

"I should know when to keep my big trap shut," Jim said with a nod.

"No, this one was on me," he replied, rubbing at the back of his neck.

Giving a smile, Jim tipped his hat and strode out of the barn.

Maddox turned back to the horse. Running a brush gently over the mare's neck and shoulders, she grew calm beneath his hands. He had much more patience with animals and the men in his military unit than he did here. At least with animals, they weren't much trouble and his unit followed orders, so not much could go wrong there. It was back here at home where his emotions got the best of him.

He was tempted to go back into the house and revoke all of Bull's spending. If he couldn't force the guy to give him all of the reins, then he'd guilt him into it. If he didn't put a stop to Bull, they were going to be out of a home. Well, Bull was, and when or if River ever came back, there wouldn't be a place to come back to.

He snorted. The likelihood of River ever coming back to the ranch was slight.

He'd seen to that.

Triton still hadn't returned. With a tip of his head, Maddox leaned back enough to glance out the door. The number three barn door still stood wide open.

"Damn it."

Once again locking the latch to the foaling stall, he headed out the door and walked across the dirt trodden path between buildings.

"I'm telling you, I didn't see anything and I won't say anything." Triton was talking to someone.

Maddox frowned and stepped into the shadowed barn. He took in several things at once. His cousin was being held between two men while a third one stood in front, pointing a gun at his cousin, and Triton had a split lip. Rage heated his skin. The fuckers had come to the wrong ranch and messed with the wrong people.

Maddox kept on advancing, his body coiled tight, his fury out for blood. One of the men glanced over and the closer he got, the more the guy's eyes widened. The one with the gun swung around, but Maddox was already on him. He gripped the gun hand, kicked out the guy's knee, and snapped the man's wrist before he snap-kicked one of the guys holding Triton in the chest. The gun went off, firing harmlessly into the side of the truck, and the man with the snapped wrist dropped, screaming on the ground.

The one he had kicked in the chest went flying back into a stack of boxes and crashed to the ground in a daze. Maddox turned on the other perp, who shoved Triton away so hard his cousin hit the side of the truck and crumbled to the ground.

"That was the last mistake you'll ever fucking make," he growled, his meaty fists clenched. The guy swung, but Maddox blocked and throat punched the man. The guy gasped and staggered back, hands flying to his throat. Keeping an eye on the screaming gunman and the one crumpled into the boxes, Maddox moved in to finish off the one in front of him.

"Mad!" He turned at Triton's cry and saw two men grabbing his cousin.

Through a red haze, two additional men ran from around the side of the truck and came at him. He punched one guy in the head, sending him to the ground. The other one swung a board and Maddox reached out and took it away one handed before he used it to beat the shit out of the guy. The other guy had rolled to his feet and a fist caught him in the jaw. He shook it off, spitting blood, and hit the guy three times in the face in rapid succession, breaking the guy's nose before the man could even blink.

"Fucker! Let go!" Triton yelled.

Something came at him from his side view and Maddox ducked, but when he came up, he miscalculated one tiny fraction and it cost him. The metal pole hit him in the side of the temple. Pain exploded through his head.

He staggered and then everything went dark.

CHAPTER FOUR

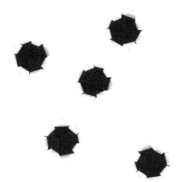

River

R IDING IN THE PASSENGER SIDE OF THE SUV WITH ISAAC behind the wheel, they left the small airport. River removed his vest and ammo belt and tossed it in the back seat. He lifted the water bottle in the center console and drank it down. Exhaustion weighed his hand down and he clumsily wiped the back of his hand against his mouth just as his private cell phone buzzed in his pocket.

"Hello?"

"River?"

"Grandpa?" River sat up a bit straighter in his seat. Surprise drew his back straight and his tiredness disappeared. He returned the look Isaac threw him. "What's the matter?"

"There's been some trouble. I need you to come home."

"What happened?"

21

"It's Maddox. He won't call you, but you need to get here. We had some trouble and he's hurt."

"Wait…Maddox? Are we talking Maddox Stone?" His stomach lurched and then soured. The SUV pulled through the gates of the base.

"Yes!" His grandfather's voice rose.

Fuck. There wasn't much if anything but a bullet that could take down Maddox Stone. Wait… why was Maddox home at the ranch?

"What happened?" He opened the door and stepped out of the vehicle. His hand hurt from gripping the phone so tightly. It took a moment before he headed toward the rear entrance. "You said he's hurt?"

"Concussion. He was jumped by some men."

"How many men?"

"A lot."

Okay, yeah, it would take a hell of a lot to take Maddox down. He swallowed through his suddenly dry throat. "Are you okay?"

"Yeah, I'm fine. I got roughed up a little." His grandfather's voice shook.

"Where was Jim? Where were the hands?" He frowned and stopped at the entrance to the barracks.

"The hands drove into Austin and spent the night. Jim was in the back pasture at the time. The hands are on their way back now."

"That's good," he said slowly, his mind racing.

"River?"

"Yeah?"

"They took Mad's cousin, Triton."

Fuck. He closed his eyes for a split second, then yanked

open the back door and stepped inside. "I'll be there in a few hours. Hang tight."

He disconnected the call and spun. Running fingers through his hair, he hurried to the nearest inside door.

"What's going on?" Isaac kept pace with him.

"I've got to go home. Something happened at my grandfather's ranch."

He strode down the hallway that would take him to the officers' quarters and offices.

He rapped on the colonel's door.

"Enter."

Stepping inside along with Isaac, he saw that Colonel Liam Cobalt wasn't alone. Blade, Diesel, Ethan, and Zane were in the office, still wearing their gear from the raid. They appeared to be waiting for them to debrief. He and Isaac walked to stand next to the others at attention in front of Liam's desk.

Liam shot him a look and then slowly narrowed his eyes. They'd known each other for years. Liam was not only his boss, but also a good friend.

"What's going on?" the colonel asked him with a frown.

"I have an emergency at home," he said abruptly. "I need to go to Texas, my family was attacked and one is missing." He rubbed at the knot forming in his sternum.

"Need backup?" Isaac asked, rubbing his hands together.

The colonel scowled and shot a dark look at Isaac. The young man snapped back to attention.

"Missing? Define missing." The colonel squinted.

"Taken against his will."

"Kidnapping on American soil is a job for the Feds."

"With all due respect, Colonel," he said, snapping his gaze to the man's, "I have some leave coming. I'd like to take it now."

The colonel narrowed his eyes. River kept his expression respectful, standing at full attention, but he knew the man could tell he was dead serious.

"Me too, Colonel," Isaac said from his spot to his right and Liam glared at the young man.

"I'll be taking mine as well," Diesel rumbled from his right.

"And I'll be -"

The colonel snapped up a hand, cutting off Blade's words.

"Pain in the asses," the man snarled, but River wasn't concerned. Liam Cobalt could be one tough son of a bitch, but one thing the man cared about as much as this unit was family.

"Tell me what you got," Liam said with a pained look accompanied by a long sigh.

"According to my grandfather, there was some type of altercation and Triton was taken against his will." He left out the part where Triton wasn't exactly blood related. That was all in the details.

Liam squinted, then tossed his pen down and leaned back in his chair. "Well, that sounds like an SAR."

"Yes, sir. It is definitely a search and rescue. I'll assess the situation when I get there."

"I'll make a note of it. I can only help so much with this." Liam scowled.

"Understood. Is there any chance I can get Wolf's help

on this?" River put it out there. Wolf was not only one of Infinity's weapons specialists, but the Captain was one of the best trackers on the planet.

"No, Wolf has enough on his plate."

"I figured." He ran a hand over the stubble on his chin, and then waited as the colonel mulled over something.

"I'll give you a week. Effective immediately, you're all on leave. God knows after that crap in Mexico, you deserve it."

Isaac gave a fist pump in the air, but then snapped back to attention when Liam shot a razor sharp glare at the man.

"If you can't resolve this in the time allotted, Lieutenant Seeger, you will be granted additional time. At that point, you'll need to reach out to the local FBI."

"Yes, sir. It shouldn't take that long."

Liam grunted and looked at the rest of the unit. "If Triton isn't found by the time your one week of leave is over, the rest of you will get your asses back here ASAP."

The room was silent, accompanied by a few nodding heads.

"Do I make myself clear?" Liam barked.

"Yes, sir!" They all replied in unison.

"You'll need transportation," Liam said decisively.

"If possible." River nodded.

"Isaac, Diesel, and Blade, collect Sam on your way out. Ethan and Zane, I need you here." Liam lifted the phone and spoke into it. He replaced the receiver.

"Wheels up in twenty."

"Thank you, Colonel."

Liam grunted. "Oh, and River?"

"Yes, sir?"

"Keep me informed at all times." Liam gave him a flat stare.

"Yes, sir."

River nodded, then spun and left the office. Everything they needed was located on this floor. He stopped by the shower room and rinsed off and changed, then grabbed his gear.

His phone rang and he sighed, recognizing the number.

"Hey," he said, catching the phone between his chin and shoulder as he zipped his duffle bag closed.

"Hey you, I'm headed to your apartment. When will you be home?" Cris asked him, and then continued before he could respond. "We need to meet up with Terry and Lorenzo at the Bistro we always eat at. Terry wants to have a baby. Well, not him, but get a surrogate for one. I don't know if Lorenzo wants one though. A kid," Cris rambled.

River shucked the backpack over his shoulder, checked the clip on his gun, and snagged the phone to hold to his ear before heading down the hallway toward the back stairs.

"I'm sorry, Cris, I'm not coming home right -" He was cut off.

"What the hell, River! You said you were coming home tonight. I thought that after we went to dinner, we could talk about things," Cris said angrily.

"Something's come up. Something important."

"More important than me?" Cris demanded. He heard the hurt in the man's voice and stopped.

"Look, it's the ranch. I'll explain once I know more."

"No, you look. I've put up with your job," Cris' voice

rose on the word job and then continued, "for years and didn't complain much. And now it's your ranch?"

The words drew him up short. The exhaustion from earlier returned and he leaned against the wall near the exit. Every damned day the man complained about one thing or another. It was forcing his hand. What he hadn't told Isaac was that he was having big misgivings about Cris. They were having trouble. He made a sound in his throat.

"Was that a snort?" Cris hissed. "Are you going back on your word?"

"What word?" he snapped, finally out of patience. He knew where this was heading. "I said I'd think about it."

"And have you?"

"Some," he stalled, really not wanting to have this conversation at the moment.

"And have you decided?" Cris demanded.

"Yes," he said very quietly. "I'm not leaving the military." He sighed and glanced toward the door that led to the stairs. "And you shouldn't have given me an ultimatum."

The silence was sudden and thick. "Okay, look."

"No." It was his turn to interrupt. "I think we need to take a break." He ran a hand over the top of his head.

"Wait. Don't do that," Cris cajoled. "Let's talk about it in person."

"I don't know if that'll do any good."

"Please."

"Okay, but I really need to go." He gently hung up the phone. Talking in person wasn't going to change the fact that Cris had drawn a line in the sand, but he needed to at least talk face to face with the man. Cris wouldn't quit until he had his say and River owed the man that much. The conversation with Cris had been coming, but he couldn't bring himself to dwell too much about it. If that made him bitter like Isaac had said, then so be it. He wasn't going to be manipulated into leaving a career he loved.

He strode out onto the roof. A black, sleek helicopter with spinning rotary blades and his team stood waiting. Jumping in, he snatched up the belt and strapped himself in before adjusting the headphones over his ears.

"I'm on an unofficial, yet official leave," Sam said with a grin and snapped on her seat belt.

"What's up, boss?" she finished.

"I have a problem at home," he replied.

"And we're gonna go fix it." Diesel cracked his knuckles from where he sat on his left.

"Let's kick some ass," Isaac huffed with a laugh from his right.

Blade and Sam were seated across from them. The two women were outstanding in their fields. Sam was their technician, and Blade was an advanced tactical weapons and combat expert. Isaac, other than being the unit's smart ass, was exceptional at unit operations and intelligence. Diesel, well, let's just say that the man resembled the name, but he was also one of the unit's engineers. The guy contained knowledge to build a freaking bridge and to blow one up if they needed. Enough said.

This wasn't the first personal mission the five of them had gone on nor would it be the last. They pretty much played it by the book, but when one of their own was involved, it changed the game. When someone fucked with his family, it changed everything.

The helicopter dropped them off at the airport and

they took a puddle jumper onto the ranch. One thing about Texas, there was enough wide open space to land a dozen planes if needed.

An SUV with the sign *Triple R* idled nearby, and the ranch foreman stepped up at their approach.

"Hello, Mr. Seeger. Welcome home."

"Hello, Jim, thank you." River smiled and shook the older man's hand with one hand and clamped his shoulder with the other.

The ranch came into view about ten minutes later. It was massive and had been in his family for four generations. The fifty thousand acre piece of land sat north of Austin. The Triple R was a working ranch. His grandfather had wanted him to stay and work the ranch after college, but college hadn't happened.

Shifting in his seat, he knew in his heart there was no place for him here now. It was all for the best though, he reminded himself. He'd joined the Army and now had a life in the unit. Everything had worked out. He drew in a calming, deep breath and eased the grip he had on his duffle bag handle. His knuckles ached a bit as he worked his fist open and closed.

The sprawling house came into view and as always, it brought a sting to his eyes. The ranch house itself was built in the mid 1800s and had been remodeled several times, the most recent one in 2015. His grandfather had mentioned it in the letters he'd received, but the man hadn't done justice describing the upgrade.

The closer they drew to the place, the more his gut tightened. So much so that he didn't hear Jim's question the first time it was asked.

"River?" Jim said again. "Will your people be staying at the house or should I make room in the bunkhouse?"

"We'll be staying at the house," he replied.

"Great," Jim said with what sounded like relief and pulled the SUV to a stop in front of the massive ranch home.

It was dark, but light from the windows shown through and the sensor light on the porch flipped on.

He lifted the duffle that held his weapons and a few changes of clothing and stepped out of the SUV. The clean Texas air hit his face and he drew in a deep breath letting it all wash over him and the fact that he hadn't been home in eight years.

CHAPTER FIVE

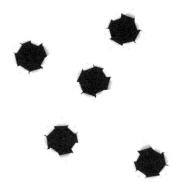

Maddox

"CAPTAIN STONE, CAN YOU HEAR ME?" A MALE VOICE SAID. He blinked and then a light was shined in his eyes. The pain was instant.

"Ah...fuck," he muttered, but then talking split his head. "Oww, goddamn it," he snarled, and then groaned.

"Take it easy," the voice said. "You've taken a hard blow to the head. Have a small sip of water."

His mouth cracked when he opened it and sucked on the straw, taking a grateful swallow of water. It took him a moment to get his throat to work, and then he took another sip before the straw was removed.

"I darkened the room so you should be able to open your eyes now," the man said.

Slowly, he blinked his lids and squinted through the slits. The low-lit room helped with his ability to focus.

"Where am I?" he croaked, having no recollection of how he had gotten there.

"County Hospital, you were brought by ambulance this morning."

His eyes finally found the man. Dr. Roberson, the guy's badge read, stood near his bed.

"Do you remember what happened?"

"I beat some asses before they hit me over the head." Some parts were missing, and he frowned and rubbed at his forehead.

The doctor smirked and frowned at the same time. "You have a concussion. I suggest you stay overnight for observation."

"Yeah. Not going to happen." He scooted up on the bed and jerked back the blankets. Stopping at that point, he gritted his teeth against the pain.

"Captain, you know I can't vouch for your health if you leave." The doctor gave him a disapproving look.

"That's okay. I don't need you to vouch for me," he muttered and carefully swung his legs over the side of the bed. "Now, if you'd get my discharge papers ready, I'll be on my way."

The man sighed and turned away.

"Wait."

"Yes?" The doctor spun back.

"Was there anyone with me in the ambulance?"

"No, but Bull Seeger called here shortly after you arrived."

"Thanks." He reached for his cell in the plastic bag of his belongings and called the ranch's number. The man didn't answer, which wasn't surprising with the way he'd left things, damn it. It was either that or Bull wasn't inside the house. The guy didn't own a cell phone, said it was too much for his seventy-eight year old mind to handle.

He suspected Bull was trying to leave him here so he'd stay overnight like the doctor wanted. Or as payback for being a dick. He left a message anyway, telling Bull he was on his way back.

"Hey, Maddox. I heard you were here," Tina, one of the ER nurses, stopped in the doorway.

"Not by choice." He smiled at his closest neighbor.

"Is it ever?" She grinned back.

He eased his foot into one of his boots. "Did Triton come into the ER?"

"No, he wasn't with you in the ambulance. Bull called, though," she said.

"I heard." He grimaced.

Tina smirked. "I'm heading out, want a ride?"

"That would be great."

It was dark by the time they made it back to the road near the ranch.

"You sure you don't want me to drive you up to the house? It's no trouble," Tina offered.

"Nah, that's okay. I need to make a phone call and the walk will give me time."

"Okay, take care, Maddox."

"You too, Tina, and thanks." He closed the door and pulled out his phone.

As if on cue, it rang.

"Stone," he clipped out into the receiver.

"Captain Stone."

He straightened. "Sir, I was just going to check in."

"How's it going at home?"

"Not so good."

He filled in Major Jones about the attack as he started

the mile walk up the gravel road that led to the ranch house. His head was a bit achy and he regretted not getting a ride up to the house now. He stopped and rubbed at the back of his head and the muscles at his neck to try and ease the tension.

"All right. We still don't have eyes on the target."

"That might work in my favor. I may not be back for a few more days." He winced and began walking again.

"Understood, I'll keep you informed."

"Thank you, sir." Maddox ended the call and shoved the phone back into his jeans.

Starting down the road again, he thought about the attack from earlier. There was way more to this than renting out a fucking barn. He and Bull were going to have it out.

He didn't know what business Bull was playing at, but it stopped now.

CHAPTER SIX

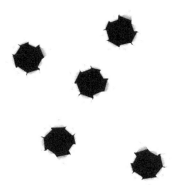

River

"**D**AMN, RIVER, YOU'VE BEEN HOLDING BACK," BLADE said, coming around from the far side of the vehicle carrying a weapons case and duffle.

"Wait until you see it in the daylight," River said with a smile.

From the outside, the place looked like a vacation lodge. With a two-story sprawling structure, the outside of the lodge was burnished wood. A large deck ran the length of the front with wide front steps leading up, covered by a large awning to keep the Texas weather at bay. Glass windows lined both the lower and upper levels of the structure to let in light or like now, reflected the interior lighting.

"River?"

Bull Seeger, his grandfather, stood at the top of the steps. The man had aged over the past eight years. Bull took a step forward with the help of a cane and River saw the bruise on the man's jaw, the cut over one eye, and the tears standing in his eyes. Anger and worry surged, hastening his steps and brought him up the stairs. Once there, River wrapped the older and somewhat frail man carefully into a hug.

He glanced around for Maddox, but there was no sign of the man, which didn't surprise him. He could imagine Maddox vehemently against him being there.

"Grandpa, what happened?" he asked once he drew back.

"Come inside." Bull turned and led the way into the great room.

"Whoa…Impressive," Isaac said, stepping through the door and into the room.

River paused just inside the door, drinking it all in. The great room was made up of thick wood beams, a cathedral ceiling, expensive furniture, hardwood floors, and a huge, red brick fireplace, one of many in the ranch.

"The rooms are on the upper levels. I can take you to them to get settled," Jim said.

"We can talk after you put your bags away," Bull said.

"I'll be right back." River nodded and took the stairs two at a time. A few moments later, he dropped his bag in his old room. The memories came back tenfold and his body went still. Before he could get sucked into recalling how happy he'd been here, he turned and made his way back down the stairs. His grandfather's cook entered the room, his face a wrinkle of worry.

"River!" Frank shook his hand.

He tightly gripped the older man's hand who'd been a friend of the family as well as their cook for the past thirty years. "Hey, Frank, how you doing?"

"Better now that you're here," Frank said hurriedly. "Ready to eat?"

"I believe we are going to talk on the front porch and then I'd love something, thanks," he replied.

"Sounds good, just holler!" Frank smiled for the first time since he'd entered and headed back through the kitchen door.

River was the first to step back out onto the front porch besides Sam. He walked to the railing instead of taking a seat. One by one, the team came out and joined him, settling in various places around the porch.

Bull thumped his way out and took a seat in an old wooden chair, resting his cane against his legs.

"Where's Maddox?"

"Maddox is on his way back," Bull said, keeping his eyes on the cane.

"From?"

"The ER."

River briefly squeezed the railing beneath his hands and then turned and slowly stepped forward. "Look at me." He waited until his grandfather lifted his eyes and held his. "Tell me everything."

"I expanded and rented out barn number three," Bull said, looking away. River rubbed at his chin, it made sense to utilize space for income, but why did his gut tell him it was more than that?

"Who do you rent it to?"

"Gillman Berk."

"The neighbor on the east side. What happened?" He frowned. He'd gone to school with Gillman Berk, the guy had been two grades behind him.

"There was an altercation about the truck. I heard a gunshot and went out there. Maddox was on the ground. Triton said he was only trying to close the door to the barn when they attacked. Mad took out six of them, I think, before one hit him in the head with a piece of pipe. I called the ambulance."

"Mad?" Isaac asked.

"Triton?" Blade asked at the same time.

"Mad is Maddox Stone, my grandfather's business partner. Triton is Maddox's younger cousin."

River looked back at his grandfather. "What's in the truck?" he asked flatly.

Bull swallowed and looked away. River waited his grandfather out. Bull looked up and took a deep breath.

"Drugs."

A crunch near the drive made him turn.

The sensor light from the porch flickered on and highlighted a man walking toward the house.

The figure took several more strides forward and then stopped with a hand raised to shield his eyes.

The sensor light illuminated US Army Captain Maddox Stone.

River tracked every step the man took as the past came rushing back. Maddox Stone had once starred in every one of his dreams. And, he reminded himself, the guy had also played a major part in empty promises and crushed hopes.

Dark hair was swept back from his forehead. Equally dark stubble ran along a powerful jaw and chin before trailing along his upper lip. If not hacked back daily, Maddox had the ability to grow a full, course yet soft beard. River rubbed his fingertips together, then clenched his fists. Standing over six feet, Maddox was pure raw muscle.

River narrowed his eyes beneath the man's perplexed stare.

∞

Maddox

Drawing near to the front of the house, the sensor light that tracked movement in the large gravel driveway flipped on.

Jerking up a hand to his pounding head, he shielded his eyes from the sudden light. *Fuck.*

From where he stood, he could make out five figures, two women and three men. One man was big, way fucking bigger than him. The other men were on the slighter side, not small, just not as big as the giant. One of the men stepped forward and he caught sight of blond hair. The other man with dark hair spun around.

It was the dark-haired one that suddenly held all of his attention.

The man stalked to the end of the porch and looked him over. Even from this distance and in the shadows of the porch, the man's muscles corded and bunched.

Not that the guy was big, because he wasn't. The man was maybe six feet, with a trim build, and there was something vaguely familiar about him. Maddox squinted, angling his hand to shade his eyes more.

The figure on the porch took one more step and the

light from the front porch illuminated the man's face. Every bit of spit dried up in his mouth and a sense of lightness filled his chest.

After eight long years, River Seeger was finally home.

Maddox could see that the years had changed River and the difference wasn't only in the power and confidence pouring from the man, or the muscles and sleeved tattoos. It showed in the man's face. A face that held a hard edge as if carved from granite. A small scar etched into the top of River's cheekbone as if life had knocked him about a bit and fashioned him into one tough son of a bitch by the looks of it, but still so smoking hot, he found it difficult to swallow.

Their eyes locked and gazes held. From this distance, River's eyes appeared coal black, but he knew the color was a rich chocolate brown shot through with specks of gold.

River at twenty had been gorgeous, but the man at twenty-eight was stunning.

"What are you doing here?" he croaked, finding his voice.

"This is my home too, if you haven't forgotten," River rasped. The man's voice had deepened, matured into a warm, rich, spine tingling baritone.

"I haven't forgotten." He cleared his throat. It was all he ever thought about.

River's nostrils flared, the man looked him over through squinted lids. River's lip curled and Maddox was left feeling like he'd come up short in some way.

Maddox took another deep breath, not sure if it was his concussion or the circumstances that were making him woozy.

Bull had told him River had gone into the military, but seeing was believing. The unit that stood next to River - and he was pretty damned sure it was a unit - appeared to be military as well. He could tell by the way they moved and strategically positioned themselves on the porch and if he wasn't mistaken, flanked the man.

What had River been up to all these years?

"You didn't answer my question, what are you really doing here?" he said slowly.

Bull's cane thumped on the porch as the older man stood and shuffled closer.

"I called him," Bull said.

"Why?" he asked Bull, but couldn't take his eyes from River.

"We're going to need the help," Bull said bluntly.

He frowned, moving up the bottom of the wide steps. "What have you done now?"

"Lieutenant?" the brown-haired woman said to River.

"Yes?" River turned away from the steps.

Maddox couldn't stop his eyes from snapping to River. The man was an officer. And even though he had nothing to do with River becoming successful, a sense of pride swelled at the man's accomplishments.

"The cook is waving at us," the woman replied.

River glanced toward the window that provided a view of the kitchen. Frank waved at them through the glass.

"Let's gather around the table," the man ordered and turned toward the front door. "Frank cooked some food, we don't want to be rude."

Maddox took a step forward, but then stopped in his tracks when the four soldiers snapped to attention and followed River into the house. It held him still for a full ten seconds. Nobody hesitated and nobody asked questions.

Maddox looked at Bull and the man lifted his shoulders, darted a look after his grandson, then shook his head and thumped his way into the house.

Releasing a long breath he didn't realize he'd been holding, he headed into the big ranch kitchen.

The men and women were gathered around the table and he took a chair at the other end from River. In the light of the kitchen, the man was even more gorgeous.

Frank filled bowls with chili and sat plates of corn bread on the thick, wood table.

"Diesel Gannon, Blade Hammond, and Sam Kimpton." River pointed to the big mountain of a man, a dark-haired woman, and a blonde woman last.

"Meet my grandfather's business partner, Captain Maddox Stone." It surprised him that River knew his full rank, but in the next moment, he realized Bull must have told him.

Maddox nodded at the others, who all held solemn expressions.

Something in River's eyes made his heart suddenly pound.

"What?"

"Someone took Triton," River said.

Every bit of blood rushed from his face. He was glad he was sitting or he might have passed out. The lump on his temple throbbed with a pain he couldn't shake.

"When?" he choked out, grabbing the edge of the table.

"Probably after you got knocked out. We've assessed

the barn. Tracks show signs of a struggle beyond your fight," a new man said, entering the kitchen and taking the chair to his left.

"Who are you?" He frowned.

"Isaac Thorne. Nice to meet you." Isaac smiled, then reached over and snagged a piece of cornbread and took a large bite.

Maddox turned his head slowly and caught Bull's gaze. "Who took my cousin?"

"It was Gillman Berk's men."

"He's dead," he said through his teeth, shoving to his feet with great effort.

"Maddox," River said abruptly.

"What?" He shot the man an impatient look.

"We get Triton back, then we can deal with Gillman."

"We? What the hell can you do?"

"Let me tell you a story first, then you decide," the dark-haired woman, the one called Blade, said.

CHAPTER SEVEN

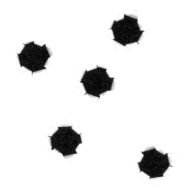

River

THE HOUSE WAS QUIET EXCEPT FOR THE OCCASIONAL MURMUR OF Diesel and Sam talking somewhere in the ranch office. Everyone else had gone to bed.

An imitation fire crackled in the hearth. The design, built by his grandfather, provided warmth in the winter and ambiance in the late spring like now. Pictures sat perched on the mantle and the smell of pine filled the air from a nearby basket of pinecones. Large mirrors hung strategically placed to make the large room appear even larger.

He ran his finger over the faces in the photos lining the mantle. Of him and Bull, and then later, him and Bull and Andrew and Maddox. Then a few of only him and a couple of him and Maddox. The county fair and the blue ribbon he'd won. The happy smile on his face as he sat perched on the gelding with Maddox standing next to him holding the reins. He'd been ten at the time, Maddox fifteen. It had taken him a year to train for the event. Maddox had been there every step of the way, tossing him back on the horse when River had wanted to quit. His eyes clung to a younger Maddox in the picture, smiling, but not at the camera. Instead, Maddox smiled up at him on the back of the horse. The sudden sting of moisture in his eyes caught him off guard and he turned abruptly away from the photo. It felt like a lifetime ago. It was most definitely another life.

Wandering over to sit in the one of the two wide, overstuffed recliner chairs next to the fire, he stared into the flames.

Maddox Stone. It felt surreal seeing him again after all these years. When he'd first left home, scared, lonely and so fucking hurt, he hadn't been able to think of anything other than Maddox. His first day of classes, he'd walked past the Army recruiting booth that sat out front of the campus and he'd enlisted on impulse.

He'd gone from there to boot camp and then training and he'd taken all that anger at Maddox out during training so that eventually, he'd thought of the man only on occasion.

Even one better, he'd avoided love like the plague and screwed around, sleeping with one man after another. It had taken his best friend, Oliver, to smack some sense into his head. That was when he'd stopped being an asshole. Or at least tried not to be so much of an asshole. From there, he'd buckled down and took classes to finish his degree and went on to Officer Candidates School in order to become an officer and one day lead his own unit. Then he'd met Cris and they'd begun dating.

Yeah, and look how that turned out?

"Hey…"

His pulse skittered and he closed his eyes at the deep, rumbling Texas drawl. Shoving to his feet, he tossed Maddox a quick glance before yanking his gaze away. Taking a few steps away from the man, he stood in the middle of the room.

"Hey," he replied and couldn't stop from briefly glancing over once more. Maddox had changed into sweats and a t-shirt that molded to his miles of muscles. His feet were bare and his hair damp from a shower. River quickly looked away and tucked his hands into his jeans.

"Infinity," Maddox drawled.

"Yeah." River nodded. "You already knew of us."

"I did. But I didn't know you were one of them."

"We can help you."

"I have no doubt."

River rubbed a hand over his head, raking back the hair that he left a bit longer on top, leaving the sides shaved, before shoving his hands back into his pockets. Once more, the flickering hypnotic flames held his attention.

"River…"

He closed his eyes, took a deep breath, braced himself, and spun.

"Yes?" He tilted his chin up and narrowed his eyes.

"It's been a long time."

"It has." His jaw clenched.

Maddox's Adams apple bobbed when he swallowed. Their eyes locked, then River glanced away. He didn't want to stare into Maddox Stone's eyes. They reminded him too much of what he'd had so long ago. Someone to hold him, be there for him, come home to. Someone to have arguments with just so they could debate about the why of it all, then kiss and make up. Maddox had been all of that to him once.

The man cleared his throat.

"I'm glad you're home."

The words stung. "Just for a few days." He hardened his voice.

"Still… I'm um…I want to -"

"Whatever you're thinking, forget it," he returned flatly, his heart thundering as he cut off the man's stumbling words.

Before Maddox could say another word, River strode across the room and jogged up the stairs. He wasn't running, he was just regrouping.

∞

Maddox

The words cut him to the quick.

His eyes clung to River's form as the soldier took the stairs upward and out of sight.

At first, Maddox couldn't believe the story Blade had told him.

River was part of a Special Forces, Black Ops military unit called Infinity. A group of men and women who were sent in to handle dangerous situations by any means necessary. Employed by the government, they were sent all over the world. Being in the military himself, Maddox had heard of the unit, but they didn't run in the same circles.

He worked solely in the Army's counter-terrorism strategy and mission's unit, while Infinity handled everything. And by everything, he meant unconventional warfare, counter-terrorism, foreign defense, and search and rescue to name only a few.

And River was one of Infinity. In fact, according to Blade, River was assistant commander for god's sake. *It's fucking impressive.* If anyone could bring Triton home, it would be Infinity.

Pulling a hand down over his mouth and chin, he gazed at the empty spot where River had quickly disappeared. What had he been thinking? That River would stay and talk to him? That everything that had happened between them would magically disappear after all these years?

"Fucking idiot," he muttered at himself.

River had every right to refuse to talk to him. Every right to not want to talk about the past. And every right to walk out on him.

He rubbed his palms on his sweats and stepped closer to the hypnotic pull of the flames in the fireplace. Once there, his gaze ran over the pictures lining the mantle. Photos of beloved days from so long ago.

The beautiful memories frozen from a time when he'd been young enough to believe love conquered all. The photos blurred and he turned away.

Here was his chance. After so many years of waiting, here was his chance to make it right with River. To try again. Only he wasn't sure how he was going to make that happen. There was so much that needed to be said. And so fucking much that he could never say.

And who's to say that River will even give you a chance? He made a sound in his throat and rubbed lightly at his temple as it throbbed. What if River did give him another chance? Would he really want to try and start a life with someone built on lies? Yet, wasn't a life built on lies better than a life without River?

It wouldn't be like he'd be lying. He just wouldn't tell him. That wasn't outright lying. *It's lying by omission.* He fisted a hand and rubbed it at the heartburn in his chest. He'd drank too much coffee again.

The fact remained that River had finally come home and it had taken a tragedy to get him there.

What would it take to make him stay?

CHAPTER EIGHT

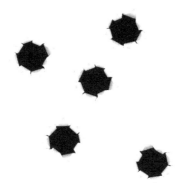

Maddox

THEY'D ALMOST LEFT HIM BEHIND. IT HAD TAKEN RIVER GIVING the big man, Diesel, a stand down nod to not have to fight them and he was grateful for that. His head hurt and Diesel was fucking huge.

It had been a sight to see the unit setup at the ranch. Infinity ran a full tactical team with a base and satellite up-link from the ranch den and deployed tactical soldiers that looked like darkly dressed warriors.

River, crouched next to his side, checked the clip of his gun and then chambered a bullet. The man was dressed in all black. A killer-looking ninja. And closed off completely. Other than a quick slicing glance, River had ignored him.

Diesel and Isaac disappeared around the corner of the building.

"Alpha team, this is Infinity base, over," Sam's voice came in clear over the mic River had handed him earlier.

"This is Alpha team, over," River responded.

"Be advised, ten possible civilians inside the building all appear to be sleeping," Sam reported.

"Roger that, base," River said and ducked down to run at a crouch to the inside wall. The man's semi-automatic was fully equipped with rapid fire and a suppressor attached. There were only two ways into the bunkhouse and they were at one of them and Bravo team the other.

"Alpha team is at the northeast main entrance," River said.

"Bravo is at the south rear," Diesel replied.

"Stay behind me," the man coldly growled the order.

Maddox narrowed his eyes, then slipped up behind River.

He placed his hand on the man's back for balance until he reached the other side. The muscles on River's back jumped beneath his palm. The man hissed and shot a look over his shoulder.

"Breach in three, two, one, go," River said tightly.

Gillman Berk's bunkhouse was dark, the men sleeping. They went in quick and quiet.

River covered a man's mouth, stuck a needle into the man's neck, and moved on. Maddox tore tape and duct-taped the ranch hands as River drugged them. They moved on to the next and then the next. Isaac and Blade moved along the other row. Diesel kept a look out. They were done before the last man ever got his eyes fully opened.

Heading out the back door, River ran in a crouch toward the foreman's cabin and Maddox followed close behind.

Reaching the door, River didn't even hesitate, he kicked it in, the splintered wood flying as it opened with a loud crack. The foreman rolled on the bed and reached for the rifle leaning on the wall next to the bed. River kicked the gun and then reached down and jerked the guy upright.

Once he had the guy on his knees, River put the end of his gun against the man heart.

"Do you know why we're here?"

The man shook his head.

River studied the guy and pressed the gun harder into the man's chest. "Did you have any part in the truck delivery at the Triple R earlier today?"

Again, the guy shook his head.

"Bullshit!" he charged hotly, taking a step forward, but stopped when River held up a hand and gave him a dark look. River turned back to the man.

"But you know about the trucks, don't you?"

"Yes," the man whispered. His eyes darted to the door, wide with fear.

"Your crew isn't coming to help you," River said conversationally and released the guy, then grabbed a chair to straddle in front of the man.

"Talk." River pulled a knife. "And if I don't like what you have to say, I'll cut off a body part." The man's eyes went wide and gazed over at him as if asking for help.

Maddox crossed his arms against his chest and scowled at the guy. "I'd rather shoot you in the nuts to make you talk, so don't look at me for help."

The man swallowed.

"They took a young man about my height, dark hair, twenty-one, bruised," River said.

"Yes," the man confirmed.

"Where are they holding him?"

"I'm not sure, but he's probably at one of three places." The guy gulped.

River jerked his head. Isaac moved and brought a paper and pen from a desk sitting nearby.

"Write the locations down," River ordered once Isaac gave the pen and paper to the foreman. The man began writing addresses.

"How long has Gillman been dealing drugs?"

The foreman looked up quickly and then down. "Wrong question." The man snorted. "When haven't they been dealing drugs."

"Is he home?"

"No, he flew into Austin tonight. Said he'll be back early day after tomorrow. He's purchasing a new bull." The man handed him the paper.

"So let me tell you what's going to happen. We're leaving. You can go release your men. Call it into the police if you feel the need or not. That's your choice if you want to deal with kidnapping charges. But if I don't find Triton at one of these locations, I'm coming back for you and no amount of cops will stand in my way," River coldly informed the man.

The foreman swallowed. Then added to the list. "There's two more. Check all five."

River stood and handed the list to him. Their fingers brushed, the touch sending his eyes roaming over River, and the paper crinkled in his suddenly tight grip.

"Let's go," the man said abruptly and stepped out onto the foreman's porch. "Regroup," River barked the order into the comm and jogged to the vehicle. The unit converged on the SUV.

Isaac got them back on the road. From where he sat,

he had a clear view of River sitting in the passenger seat, but the man deliberately didn't look his way.

He doesn't care to look.

Maddox pulled at the hairs along his chin and turned to gaze out the window. The vehicle bounced when they went from dirt to pavement and he grimaced slightly and lifted a hand to his head.

"Here." Blade held out a couple of aspirin and a bottle of water when he turned.

"Thanks," he said, taking the pills and drinking all the water.

"No problem. I've had a few concussions in my time."

Diesel leaned over the center console and started a conversation with River about strategies.

"You guys go way back?" he asked Blade quietly, pulling his gaze away from River.

"All of us have been together five years," she said.

The way the unit moved, he could believe it.

"What's your role?"

"Weapons," Blade said with the corner of her mouth tipping in a slight smile.

"And River?"

"Well, he does everything. I mean, we all cross train, but River? The lieutenant takes it to a whole other level." Blade grew serious.

Maddox couldn't help but glance toward River again.

"You respect him." It wasn't a question.

"Any one of us would gladly follow him through the gates of hell."

∞

River

The first two places had been a bust. They had three more to go.

He uncapped a water bottle and poured it over his head and shook his hair out.

The warm hand against the small of his back had left a lingering heat in its wake and he hoped he didn't look as flushed as his face felt right then thinking about it. How was he going to make it through this? There was no way in hell he would be sucked back into Maddox Stone's life. No fucking way could he be that stupid. He made a sound in his throat and guzzled the rest of the water before he capped it and tossed it into the nearby trash.

Turning, he found his arm caught.

"What?" He slanted the man an irritated look.

"Apparently, you don't know what I do for a living," Maddox said in that deep Texas drawl.

Although only a foot separated them, River stepped closer to make his point. "I know exactly what you do for a living, Captain, but this is my mission. I give the orders," he rasped across the small space between them. Maddox had a few inches on his six foot one frame, causing his head to tip back in order to meet the man's turbulent blue gaze.

"If you can't accept that then you can sit home," he said between his teeth, leaning in a bit more until their faces were inches apart. Maddox's chest rose and fell a bit more rapidly.

"The hell I'll sit home," the man returned huskily, eyes roaming over his face and dropping to his mouth.

"Then I suspect we have a deal," he replied abruptly and stepped back.

It was a standoff for a long moment. Finally, Maddox gave a slow nod.

With a pounding heart, River took another step away. *Shit.* He took one additional step away before resting his back against the SUV, but even distance couldn't stop his body from buzzing. He crossed his arms and silently kicked himself in the ass. He cursed his own stupidly for putting himself inside the man's personal space. River typically did that with his men when he wanted to make a point, and he'd done it unconsciously. His mind had forgotten how Maddox's closeness affected him, but his cock damn well hadn't.

Maddox continued standing at his right and River tried not to look directly at the guy. But turning his eyes away didn't take away the tingling of awareness that lingered. He'd known Maddox his whole life, of course there was still going to be awareness between them!

For years, it had been only him and Bull, until Maddox. River had been raised by his grandfather when his parents decided they'd rather travel the world than raise a son. As an only child, his only living relative, Bull Seeger, had claimed him immediately. He remembered clearly when Bull went into business with Andrew Stone the year River had turned nine. That was the year that was forever etched into his memory, the year he'd met Maddox, Andrew's grandson. From that day forth, he'd spent most of his adolescence tagging along after the fourteen year old and hanging on his every word.

"You've worked many cases like this before?" the man asked gruffly, pulling back his attention.

"Yes." Finding his control again, he gazed off in the distance.

"Successful?"

"He's been gone less than twenty-four hours, there's a good chance he's still alive."

"You didn't answer me. Successful?"

"Yes, Maddox. We're excellent at what we do," he said, flicking his eyes to the man.

"Thank you," Maddox murmured, and then lifted a hand to his head and swayed.

Before he could think twice, River snapped a hand out to close around Maddox's bicep. "Let's go." He opened the SUV and urged the man carefully inside the back seat, kicking himself in the ass for forgetting that Maddox was still nursing a concussion.

"I'll drive," Diesel told Isaac, and the pair changed places.

"Can we get some food?" Isaac asked.

"Yes," Maddox spoke quietly. "Food sounds good."

"Let's stop at the diner outside of town. I don't want to bring attention to ourselves," he agreed, running his eyes over Maddox's tired face.

They reached the diner. His crew removed their vests and gear, leaving them in black tactical pants and t-shirts, and they entered the diner with Maddox.

"Want anything?" Isaac called out.

"How about a one way ticket away from here?" he wanted to shout.

"No," he called out.

"I'll bring you a burger." Isaac grinned.

He snorted and pulled out his phone.

Liam answered on the first ring.

"Fill me in."

He made it brief, but gave Liam all the details.

"You think your grandfather is telling you the whole truth?"

"Caught that did you?"

"Yeah. He knows they're storing drugs on your property and not much else? Why do I get the feeling there is way more to that story?"

"Because I'm sure there is. Hopefully, we'll come home with Triton here soon and I can get the rest out of gramps."

"What if you don't find Triton at the remaining sites?"

"Then I have a feeling my grandfather might know where he's being held."

"You think he's a part of this?"

"Not like you think, but he might know something that he doesn't realize he knows."

Boots approaching on the gravel had him turning sideways to lean against the vehicle. Maddox walked toward him, long strides eating the distance between them. The man wore black boots and tight jeans with a t-shirt that strained over his muscles. Lean hips filled out those tight blue jeans, and he had that fucking cowboy hat. A black one that was sexy as fuck. He spun away when Maddox caught him staring at his crotch.

"Need additional back up?"

"You mean more people on unofficial official leave?" he teased, anything to get his mind off the man at his side.

"Yes, smart ass," Liam said with a chuckle.

"I might. I'll text you if I do."

"River?" his boss said before he could hang up.

"Yeah?"

"Be careful."

"Always am," he grunted and hung up.

Maddox held out the burger and he took it, careful to keep his fingers from touching the other man's. Tearing off the paper, River ate it standing near the passenger door. Juice dripped onto the dirt near his boots. Maddox handed him a napkin and he took it and wiped his mouth.

He kept his eyes on the burger and continued to eat quickly. The faster they got back on the road, the sooner they could get this shit done, because he was leaving at the end of the week or sooner if they found Triton.

"You're on leave?"

"Yeah. I had some coming," he said around a mouthful of food, watching the way tiny lines crinkled at the corners of Maddox's eyes when he was thinking something over or the way the muscles on the man's chest bunched when he crossed his arms.

The rest of the team came out of the diner and saved him from making a fool out of himself and blurting out the only thing he could think of right then. *Why had Maddox sent him away?* After the team jumped into the SUV, they had one more moment alone.

"We better head out." He wadded up the bag and tossed it into the nearby trash.

Maddox reached out and grasped his bicep and River stilled.

"I…"

The man's words dropped away. River whipped his head around, heat skittered along his skin beneath the man's touch.

Maddox closed his mouth, opened it, and then closed it again. River tipped his head, trying to read the man's expression.

"You?" He drug out the word and scowled, sudden quickfire anger replaced his foolish thinking and his mouth suddenly replaced any semblance of decorum. "What? Missed me? Regret not meeting me on that train platform?"

Maddox's eyes glittered in the morning light with a blue that rivaled the sky around noontime. The man was struggling to say something.

"It's okay, Maddox. It's all in the *past*." He ground the words out and narrowed his gaze. "We'll get Triton back, I'll get my grandfather in line, and we can go back to the way it was."

"Is it still in the past, though?" Maddox's brow furrowed, a look of sadness in his blue eyes.

Like a slap in the face, the quiet words bothered the fuck out of him, but he wasn't going to show it to this man. He tucked away every bit of anger and hurt and settled a cold mask over his face and eyes. His ability to close off his emotions had served him well in the past.

"Yes." He tugged his arm from the man's grip and stepped up into the passenger seat.

"All right, boss?" Diesel's deep voice rumbled.

"Yup. What's next on the list?"

CHAPTER NINE

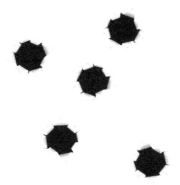

River

H E TOOK THE STAIRS TWO AT A TIME. MADDOX HAD GONE IN before he could even get the SUV turned off. The cowboy was spitting mad. Shouting barreled through the house the minute he shoved the door open.

Three locations had been a bust. Still two to go. It worried him, but the anger coming from the front room worried him more and he hastened his steps.

"I want answers and I want them now! Why the hell did you allow drugs to be kept on our property?" Maddox bellowed.

River entered the room at a run and found the man towering over Bull. The older man shrank back in his chair, fingers white clasping the chair arms.

"I'm sorry!" Bull cried.

"You turned our place into a drug stop, my cousin is kidnapped, and you're sorry?" Maddox snarled.

"Maddox," he said sharply.

"What!" The man spun on him.

"Let him talk," he said calmly.

Maddox glared at him, gnashed his teeth, and then stomped over to take a seat in the chair next to the one Bull was sitting in.

"Tell us what happened from the beginning," River said to his grandfather, taking a seat on the couch in front and across from the two chairs. "And don't leave anything out."

The rest of the Infinity gathered around.

Bull sank back in the wide, overstuffed chair. "It all began when your grandmother got sick with cancer. We didn't have any insurance. About twenty years ago, I borrowed fifty thousand dollars from Larry Berk, that's Gillman Berk's father. Larry didn't collect on the debt for a long time."

"Did my grandfather know about the debt?" Maddox cut in.

"No, Andrew never knew," Bull said.

"Go on," Maddox growled.

"About eight years ago, Larry finally called to collect on the debt. I told him I didn't have that kind of money, so he said I could do him a few favors. At first, it was keeping small packages that I'd pick up in town and put them out in the tool shed and Larry would send someone over to pick them up."

"How did it turn into a truck delivery?" River asked.

"When Larry passed away, Gillman took over. He's meaner and more ruthless than his father."

River waited and Bull continued.

"Gillman started stashing a truck here instead of me picking up packages. I knew the truck contained drugs, so I put him in the far pasture and never told Maddox. Then Gillman wanted to store the truck inside, said it wasn't safe out in the open. So I took out a loan to expand the barn to accommodate him. That's when Triton called Maddox about the account going negative and the bills not being paid."

"Why did the account go negative if you took out a loan?" River frowned.

"Because not only had I taken out the loan for the barn expansion, I was giving Gillman money to pay off the rest of the debt I owed his father. I thought if I paid him quickly, it would get him the hell off our land quicker." Bull sighed.

"When do they deliver the trucks?" Maddox frowned.

"Several times a month. One guy leaves the truck. A few days later, another one comes to pick it up," His grandfather said, then took a breath but stopped and looked away.

"What? Tell us everything." River kept his tone hard.

"Gillman and I weren't the only ones that knew about the trucks coming and going."

"Who else knew?" Maddox growled.

"Damon Reding, the guy who hangs out with Triton's boyfriend, Clay. Somehow, he found out."

"What did he do?" River narrowed his eyes on Bull.

"He started sending some of his men to take some of the drugs from Gillman's trucks. When I confronted Reding about it, he said that Gillman knew all about it. But I knew he was lying."

"Who's Damon Reding?" Maddox thrust agitated fingers through his hair.

"A drug dealer that runs a small time street gang out of Austin. Some of the hands had a run in with him a few weeks back," Bull said. "They'll tell ya, he's a mean SOB."

"Where's the truck now?" River asked his grandfather.

"It was stolen by Reding and his gang yesterday while you were in the ER," Bull told them.

"Do you think that Reding has Triton?" River asked.

"No. Gillman has Triton."

"Explain," Maddox snapped.

"Like I said, I heard the gun shot and went out to the barn. Maddox was knocked out. Damon and his crew hit me and took the truck."

"And?" River pushed, narrowing his eyes when his grandfather paused.

"After the ambulance came and took Maddox to the hospital, Gillman's men showed up. When they saw the truck was gone, they took Triton. Said they'd only give him back when I gave them the truck back with everything in it." Bull rubbed a gnarled hand at his mouth.

"You're just telling us now?" Maddox shouted and stood, fists clenched.

River stood as well.

"I didn't mean for any of this to happen! I swear. I only needed the money for Mary. I didn't know how to pay it back." Bull broke down and cried.

Maddox turned and quietly walked out of the room.

River growled beneath his breath and spun on his grandfather. He steeled himself against Bull's tears, he'd be no help to the older man if he got caught up in Bull's emotion. The elderly man took another moment to collect himself.

River ran a hand over his mouth and chin, holding his grandfather's gaze.

"I get why you took the money from Larry. What I don't understand is why you would risk everything by doing something shady to pay the money back."

"I was afraid. I didn't know what to do. I never meant for anyone to get hurt."

A crash sounded in the kitchen. River closed his eyes against the pain of Maddox cursing.

"I'll see how he is." Blade headed that way.

For a brief moment, River held a hand over his mouth, feeling the stubble on his jaw.

"What's the plan, boss?" Isaac inquired.

"I have a pretty good idea," River said, thinking quickly.

"Are you thinking what I'm thinking?" Isaac gave a slight grin.

"I think I am." River nodded.

"I know I fucking am," Diesel growled.

"What? What are you thinking?" Bull asked from his chair.

Maddox and Blade came back from the kitchen. River held Maddox's gaze across the distance.

"What's the plan?" Maddox asked quietly.

"How do you feel about robbery?"

CHAPTER TEN

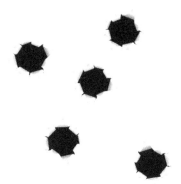

Maddox

THE QUIET REACHED HIM FIRST, THEN THE SOUND OF EVEN LOW voices and his eyes snapped open and he jerked upright.

"Oww, fuck." He grabbed at his head before glancing around.

Four faces were watching him. He met and held River's dark, smoldering gaze. A sudden shutter seemed to come down over the man's eyes and Maddox felt effectively locked out as if a door had slammed shut in his face.

"How long was I out?" he croaked.

"About thirty minutes."

"You waited?"

"We power napped," Diesel said, and Isaac chuckled.

"You should have woken me." He frowned at River.

"It wouldn't have done any good. We needed to wait for dark. It was a good time to shut our eyes for a few minutes." River's tone was remote, detached.

Other than the brief second earlier, River barely looked at him now when he spoke. It had begun back at the confrontation of sorts beside the SUV at the diner.

One minute, River was all up in his space making a point and mocking him about the past, and the next thing, the man was as cold as an arctic wind. The guy had shut him out in a matter of seconds, showing clearly that he couldn't be bothered with the past or him.

Which sucked because finding River on his front porch had tilted his whole fucking world.

"Are we calling for reinforcements, boss?" Isaac asked.

His head snapped up and Maddox winced, lifting a hand to rub at the back of his neck. Reinforcements?

"I sent the colonel a text message. He's sending out two more of the team. We can't be in three places at once," River replied.

"Colonel?" he asked.

"Colonel Liam Cobalt," Diesel replied.

He'd heard of the colonel. The man's reputation proceeded him. Cobalt was powerful yet known to be easy going except when pushed, then god help that person. He could definitely see why Colonel Cobalt was in charge of Infinity.

"What's the plan?" He stood.

River tipped his head as if working it all out in his head.

"We'll send the team in twos to check the last two addresses for Triton." River's tone was short, then he turned away and headed for the door.

Maddox ground his teeth, grabbed his jacket, and hurried to follow.

"You, me, Isaac, Blade, and Diesel will go to Reding's

place and get the truck back," River said as he stepped outside. "And whoever the colonel sends will take over the other two locations."

"What if Gillman kills Triton?" Maddox questioned, jogging to catch up.

"They won't. Gillman wants his drugs back. If he is going to kill Triton, he'll wait to do it until you bring him the truck. Then he'll try and kill you both," River told him.

"How can you know that?"

"It's what I would do," River said with a hard, flat tone.

Oh, that's right, the cold, methodical soldier was here to do a job.

For a moment, he'd forgotten who he was speaking to.

Before he could question River further, Jim pulled up in a second ranch SUV. River strode over and pulled off each Triple R magnetic sticker that was on the two front doors and tossed them into the back.

Diesel carried several large bags, which looked like body bags, and stuffed them into one of the SUVs. The man gave a thumbs up, got into the vehicle, and started the engine.

Maddox grabbed River's wrist before the man could get into the other SUV. This was the third time he'd grabbed the guy, but for some reason, he couldn't stop reaching for him.

River tensed and then looked at him, eyes unreadable.

"Thank you."

"You're welcome. Now, let's go get that truck." River pulled away.

Damn it. He frowned. The River he'd known before had been emotional and full of curiosity and life. A younger River hadn't been able to shut off his emotions like this. He'd met the man when his grandfather bought into the Triple R. He'd run on the ranch as a young boy dodging fists, riding horses, and listening to his grandfather's stories, all with River tagging along at his side. The boy had talked nonstop. So different than this cold and stoic stranger.

Disappointment held Maddox still for a moment and then he took a deep breath and let it out before getting into the back of the SUV. Diesel followed them in the second vehicle. Maddox took a minute to lean his aching head back. The tires on the road hummed.

"You know you can't mount like that, right?" He shook his head at the short nine year old sitting on a fence railing trying to get his leg over the rump of a horse.

It was an awkward position that looked like an accident waiting to happen.

"I can too!" the kid said and blew the bangs out of his face. River was all eyes, curly hair, and flashing smile. "Just you watch."

The boy hiked his leg and grabbed the saddle just as the horse took two steps forward. River slipped and Maddox grabbed ahold of the kid and tossed him up into the saddle.

"Watch what? You break your neck?" he laughed.

River grinned down at him and raced away on the back of the large red horse.

He jerked upright when the SUV hit a pothole in the road, the small memory of their childhood fading. River had lived in a bubble thinking nothing on earth could hurt him. In contrast, Maddox had been born into a life of pain and betrayal.

He shifted and glanced out the window. Perhaps the sooner they found Triton and the sooner he left, the better off everyone would be.

⎯⎯⎯

Damon Reding had a few men standing guard around the shed and garage. Most of the men stayed tucked up against the house, talking or smoking. None were patrolling, which worked in their favor. They parked across the field from the house and used binoculars to keep surveillance.

"Looks like Damon's got a small army," he said.

"Mhmm," came the unresponsive reply.

"So, we're going to Gillman's after we get the truck?" Maddox gave an annoyed sound in the back of his throat.

River turned in his seat and held his gaze for a moment. "According to the foreman, Gillman is still in Austin."

"We can give him a welcome back party then." He wanted nothing more than to get his hands on Gillman.

"We can't enter Gillman's house yet," River said.

"Why not?" Maddox clench his jaw.

"Because they have a state of the art security system, armed guards, and there aren't enough of us. Once my men get here and I send them to check on the other locations for Triton, we'll have more options," River said, and returned to looking through a set of binoculars.

"What options?"

"One option is my team will recover Triton and we can take the truck to the local authorities and have

70

Gillman arrested. Or two, they don't recover Triton and we take the truck to Gillman and do the exchange."

The next second, River had replaced the binoculars with a gun that was pressed against the glass of the driver's side window.

A large man stood outside the door with a cocky grin on his very handsome face.

"Damn it, Zane, you're going to get yourself killed," River growled after opening the window.

"It's all good." The big muscled man smiled.

River snorted. "I do not want Diesel gunning for me the rest of my life."

Zane's chuckle was a low rumble. "I doubt he'd do that."

River shook his head. "Right."

When River exited the vehicle, Maddox followed.

"Zane, this is Maddox Stone. It's his cousin who was taken."

"Maddox, this is Sergeant Zane Gannon, Diesel's younger brother."

Zane nodded seriously. "We'll get him back."

"Thank you, Sergeant." Maddox was touched at the sincerity.

"Bah, just call me Zane. Technically, I'm on vacation."

Maddox couldn't wrap his head around the fact that all these men had taken leave to come help River.

River gave Zane the coordinates to the two remaining hostage sites. Zane headed toward his brother Diesel and collected the keys of the second SUV.

Maddox looked in the direction Zane had gone.

"Zane's an expert. He and his team will check the two

other locations." The way River said it, Maddox had no doubt.

"And if he finds Triton?"

"He'll call me," River responded.

"You said you've done this before."

"Yes. And I know you do something similar, Captain Stone," River said, eyeing him.

He shook his head slowly. "Not really." His unit was not on the same level with Infinity.

"We run in the same circles." River squinted at him.

"Do we?" He arched one eyebrow.

"My team and I were actually really close once."

"What? How close?" He blinked in surprise.

"Ever ask yourself who got called in for Jamal?"

His heart thundered. Holy fucking Christ. Jamal, the terrorist, the close call in Mali. Maddox's unit had been set to do the mission, but then they'd broken out with a nasty case of the flu, leaving them on the sidelines.

The unit that replaced them had been fast and fucking good. Four darkly dressed men arrived on location. A unit who had only been seen through surveillance cameras. Men who had taken the terrorist out and then disappeared.

He rubbed at his upper lip. Now he understood why he'd studied one of the men dressed in all black more than the others. The walk, the way he moved, had drawn him. Maddox had examined the film over and over. So much so, his team had razzed him about having a crush.

"That was you…"

"I told you we run in the same circles."

He held the man's eyes for a few moments, then turned away.

Shoving his churning disappointment onto the back burner, Maddox pulled his gun to check the clip. *Perhaps this was life's payback? A slug to the gut that said it all.* River had been that close two years ago and hadn't bothered to say a word.

CHAPTER ELEVEN

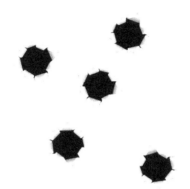

Maddox

H UNKERED DOWN IN THE WARM TEXAS NIGHT, HE GLANCED AT
the man at his side. River was calm and in control
with his orders and methodical plan. The man had
been nothing but cool toward him.

"Alpha team, be advised vehicle approaching from the
east," Sam said.

"Copy that," River murmured and lifted the binoculars. Maddox lifted his own. A car pulled up and a woman got out with three bodyguard types and entered the
residence.

"Bravo, what's your position?" River asked.

"Entering one of the back barns," Diesel replied.

"Just about there, boss," Isaac said, the other half of
Bravo team.

"Roger, Bravo, let me know when you locate that
truck."

Silence reigned over the cool Texas night. While the days could be hot as hell, the nights were still cool.

"Alpha team, truck has been located. Diesel is behind the wheel," Isaac responded after several minutes.

"Roger that, mission is a go," River said and ran in a crouch across the field. Maddox, along with Blade, followed the man.

"Roger, Alpha team," Sam echoed.

"Ready?" River murmured, shifting closer, and Maddox drew in a deep breath of the man's clean spicy scent. *Fuck*.

"Yeah," he rasped.

River lifted his night vision goggles into place and moved out. The sound of gunfire followed, men shouted, a woman screamed, and people ran through the night.

They took out the two men standing guard. Knocked them out, zip-tied hands, and duct-taped mouths shut.

It wasn't a fair fight, criminals and drug users against a military unit. It lasted about fifteen minutes max. In the end, Damon Reding and three of his men were dead. The woman and the rest of the house's occupants were zip-tied and left waiting for local law enforcement. A few of Reding's men ran for the desert.

Under the cover of darkness, River and his unit placed the body of Damon Reding and his three men in body bags and then into the back of the big rig truck.

"Why?" Maddox asked gruffly.

"It's a message for Gillman letting him know we don't tolerate drug dealers," Isaac said, cinching the body bags closed to keep the bodies hidden.

"But these aren't Gillman's men." He frowned.

"That doesn't matter. They're dead drug dealers," Blade said. "It will get the message across."

River reported the drug house to the sheriff's office. There were enough people and evidence inside the house to keep investigators busy for a while.

They sped through the night, leading the way in the black SUV with Diesel driving the truck. They entered the Triple R property by way of the north gate.

With the fifty thousand acre spread, there was plenty of places to hide the big rig. Maddox personally knew every inch of the steep hills they were headed toward.

River pulled beneath a cluster of trees that had previously been used as a camp site. Diesel followed and then drove the truck further on to park beneath a dozen trees that surrounded one of the watering holes.

Unfolding a massive camouflage netting, the crew pulled it up and over the box trailer.

"Came with the truck," Blade told River.

The SUV was unloaded and he realized they were making camp. Tents were thrown up and multiple fold-out burlap chairs were set around a fire pit with large rocks. Some of the team gathered wood and others cooked the food.

"Won't they see the fire?" Isaac asked.

"No. We're too far out," he told the man.

"So, now we wait." Diesel rubbed his hands together.

"Keep that fire contained," River ordered. "I want water nearby. As soon as food's cooked, put it out."

A vehicle approached from the north and lurched down the deeply grooved access road.

Maddox pulled his gun and checked the clip.

"It's Elijah," River said from his side.

Maddox hadn't even heard the man approach. He glanced over and tipped his head slightly and after a moment, he tucked his gun away. Not sure who Elijah was.

Zane stepped out from the back of the SUV and lifted gear from the seat. Another man exited the driver's side. A woman with dark black hair hopped out of the passenger side and strode at the man's side. She wore tight, black leather, a gun at one hip, and some type of knife that looked like a short sword hanging on her other hip.

"Lieutenant Seeger," Elijah said to River on approach.

"Captain Cobalt, this is Captain Maddox Stone, it's his cousin who's missing," River made the introductions.

Elijah shook his hand.

"Hello, Captain." The woman introduced as Pia Rozario gave him a nod.

"Call me Maddox," He threw River a dark look at the sudden use of his title. They weren't on a military mission. This was personal. He returned the woman's nod with one of his own.

Zane approached and dropped his bags in the dirt. "There was no hostage at the two remaining properties," Zane told them.

Maddox rubbed at his chest and shoved down his worry.

"We'll do a trade with Gillman when he gets back from Austin in the morning," River said.

Maddox spun away and gazed out into the Texas night where the moon sent a glimmer over the dark terrain. *Where the hell was his cousin?*

∞

River

"Don't want to be called Captain?" he asked, squinting at the man after the others had walked away.

"No, this isn't a military mission." Maddox rubbed at the back of his neck and glanced away.

When Maddox kept his face turned away from him, River gritted his teeth. "Okay. You should get some rest," he said abruptly and shoved his hands deep into his pockets and spun, heading toward Elijah.

"River." Elijah turned from grabbing his duffel bag.

"Elijah, thanks for helping."

"No problem. Happy to help. Plus, I needed some R and R."

River smiled at his friend and younger brother of Colonel Liam Cobalt.

His phone rang, taking his attention from Elijah, and he walked a few yards away.

"Colonel."

"River," Liam replied. "Fill me in."

"This is turning out bigger than I anticipated."

"Are Elijah, Pia, and Zane on site?"

"Yes, thank you."

"Is that enough help?"

"Let me tell you what we're up against and then you tell me." He filled Liam in on what was happening. They had the ranch to protect, the truck full of drugs to guard, Triton still missing, and Gillman was due back from Austin tomorrow where they were set to do an exchange.

"Hmmm. I'll send a few more."

"Thanks, Colonel. Tell whoever you send that I'll have

the ranch Foreman, Jim, pick them up and bring them to where I am."

"Will do." Liam hung up.

Keeping his gaze from seeking out Maddox, River headed over to the fire and squatted next to the smoldering coals left doused by buckets of water. Leaning forward, he snagged one of the grilled hot dogs still sitting on the grill and took a bite.

"What's the word, boss?" Blade asked.

River wiped at his mouth, swallowed, and spoke. "The colonel is sending a few more of the unit. I'll have Jim bring them out here."

"Oooh," Isaac said. "Things are gonna get real now."

River nodded. *Damned real.*

Liam sent Oliver, Ethan, and Dillon.

He smiled when his best friend made a beeline for him.

"What the hell? I know I was in the field, but to take off and not call me?" Oliver groused.

River returned the man's hand clasp. Oliver Rains was his best friend and had been since army boot camp. They'd been in the same Special Forces unit before being recruited by the colonel to join Infinity.

"I know. I took off quickly and I figured you'd text me when you were in a good place."

"True that," Oliver grinned. "Plus, I'm on some type of bogus military leave." The cute, young man snicker snorted.

River chuckled. "Guess the boss figures the more people he throws at the problem, the sooner he'll get his unit back."

"Guess so." Oliver laughed. "So…How'd the boyfriend take it?" the man stage whispered.

River grimaced.

"Does Cris know what he's asking you to give up?" Oliver pressed.

"Don't start." He frowned at his friend.

"Somebody needs to. You're only twenty-eight, you have a lot more years."

"I know." River smiled and gripped Oliver's shoulder. "I told him no, but he wants to talk about it when I get home."

Oliver snorted, looked around, and then snapped his head back toward him.

"Is that Maddox?" his friend whispered.

Glancing in the direction Oliver had, he spotted Maddox. After his outburst about the damned train station, he'd been cool toward the man.

He suspected Maddox wanted to talk. River would give the man a chance to explain. What River didn't want were some snatches of conversation between gun fights or when they happened to stop by the ranch for twenty minutes to shower. No, when they talked, he didn't want them interrupted. So talking would need to happen after Triton was found.

River wanted answers, and he suspected that digging it out of Maddox might take them a while. Because just like in the past, when Maddox wanted to talk about something, the man was having trouble spitting it out.

"Yeah, that's Maddox." He ran his gaze over the man crouched next to the fire, eating.

River had needed to share with at least one other human being and since Oliver was his best friend, he was the one that had been there for him in the beginning.

"Want me to punch him in the mouth?" Oliver offered.

River smirked, taking in the five foot ten inch Oliver with his dark, curly hair and smiling eyes.

"I wouldn't try it."

"Really?" his friend said with raised brows.

"Yeah. Trust me. I know you're trained. But so is he. His team was set to take Jamal before we were called in."

"No shit?" Oliver looked at Maddox, and River noted the new respect in his friend's gaze.

"And I'd appreciate if you'd be nice to him."

"What the fuck? Why?" Oliver's gaze snapped back to him.

He turned away from the probing gaze.

"I want a chance to talk to him to get some fucking closure," he growled.

Oliver snorted. "Riiiight."

He turned and stared at his best friend until Oliver held up his hands. "Okay, that makes sense. Get some closure so you can both walk away without that shit between you. Plus, you have the *crybaby* at home waiting."

He gave a tired sigh. "Don't call Cris that."

Oliver snapped his fingers. "Oh yeah, that's right! Let's forget Cris asked you to choose." Oliver made a face at his glare. "But still, it's good to get *closure*," his friend added with air quotes.

"Exactly," he replied, ignoring Oliver's mocking tone.

Their conversation was interrupted by the approach of Dillon and Ethan.

River shook hands with Dillon, who he hadn't seen since the man had been on a mission with Oliver.

He fist bumped Ethan. "Thanks for coming," he said.

"Of course. Does Sam have the layout of Gillman's place?" Ethan asked.

"Yes, she's set up a base at Triple R. I'll show you what she sent me." He spun and headed to the opened end of the SUV where Elijah stood. River reached out and, flipping a lap top around, he showed Ethan the inside layout of Gillman Berk's estate.

"Let's gather around," Elijah ordered.

They all clustered around the SUV. Elijah mapped out the details of the trade tomorrow. They'd hit the estate be-fore dawn. The plan was to get Triton out of there before giving Gillman the truck.

"What's that?" Elijah jerked his chin at the body bags after inspecting the contents of the truck.

"A message, sir," Diesel told the captain.

The man smirked. "All right, get some rest," the man said, and moved off toward the campfire. Ethan and Zane followed their leader, flanking him.

He slipped into the front driver seat of the SUV and hit the lever to recline it back. Oliver slipped in the other side and did the same.

"Think the kid is still alive?"

"Yeah. This guy wants his drugs back. Plus, he probably thinks once he gives Triton back, things will go back to the way they were."

"Storing drugs on your property, not fucking likely." Oliver pulled his hat low over his forehead.

"Borrow that?" He grinned at the hat.

"Damn right," Oliver laughed with closed eyes. "I'm no cowboy."

CHAPTER TWELVE

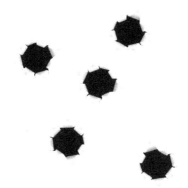

River

THEY PARKED THE TRUCK FILLED WITH DRUGS ON AN OLD DIRT road that butted up against Gillman Berk's property.

He cinched his vest and pulled on his helmet and adjusted his ear piece before glancing at the rest of his Alpha team, which consisted of Elijah, Dillon, and Maddox.

Maddox was dressed in fatigues, vest, ammunitions belt, boots, and a tactical helmet with a semi-automatic grasped in his strong hands. They wore almost the same attire only his was completely black while Maddox's had some dark camouflage. Maddox glanced up and gave him a quiet, searching look.

River swallowed and pulled his gaze away to study the layout of the area.

"Infinity base, this is Alpha team," he said roughly, testing the mic.

"Roger, Alpha team," Sam said. "Bravo? Charlie team?"

"Bravo team in position," Isaac whispered, who was with Blade and Pia.

"Charlie team ready," Oliver murmured, who was with Ethan.

Zane and Diesel had stayed back to guard the big rig truck.

"Be advised movement in the northeast stairwell," Sam said. The technician previously hacked into the home's security camera system and was utilizing it against Gillman.

"Charlie team, you close?" River murmured.

"On it," Oliver grunted.

River lifted the night vision binoculars and caught sight of Oliver and Ethan creeping through the dark toward the northeast corner of the estate-like home that sat back on Gillman Berk's ranch.

"You got that alarm shut off, base?" Elijah rasped into the mic.

"One more moment, Captain," Sam replied.

River rocked in his boots where he stayed squatted down out of sight near one of the smaller outbuildings that stood north of the main house. Getting into a better position, River jerked his head toward Maddox and sprinted across the short expanse of land to a water tower. Beneath the water tower sat a large, old, unused propane tank. He crouched and felt Maddox on his right and then Dillon on his left.

The bunkhouse sat away from the main house, so it had been easy to neutralize Gillman's hands. Mostly, because the building had been vacant except for five men. They'd wake up with headaches, but at least they'd wake up. Most of the men appeared to be positioned around the house itself.

"This is Charlie team. The movement is two hostiles at the top of the stairwell," Oliver said.

"Roger that, Charlie, sit tight," River responded. Another few minutes went by.

"Infinity leader, the alarm is deactivated," Sam responded.

"Mission is a go," Elijah said into the mic, coming up on his flank.

Charlie and Bravo teams were in position, guarding all exits to prevent runners.

He tossed a rope and tied it off to the upper balcony. Rapidly pulling himself upward, he climbed over the railing. Maddox came next, then Elijah and Dillon.

River slipped across the expanse of the balcony and took out his tools. Quietly, he picked the lock and opened the door, then entered into what looked to be a brightly colored girl's bedroom. He hadn't been expecting that. It took him off guard for a moment, but then he stepped farther inside, searching for occupants. The room stood empty.

Elijah nodded to the stuffed animals on the bed. "Even drug lords have families."

"Watch out for little ones," Maddox murmured, and the others nodded.

Stepping out of the bedroom door, he turned to the right and advanced, gun up. Lights were on below. Taking the stairs downward on silent feet, he stopped at the edge of an archway to a large front room with the rest of Alpha team by his side.

"I know you're there!" A voice called out.

"Gillman Berk?" Elijah called back.

"Yes!" Gillman shouted back.

"We want to talk. We have your truck," the Captain answered.

"Okay, come out slowly," the man said. He didn't tell them to drop their guns.

River dodged a quick look into the room and saw a group of men before ducking back. The room was massive with wide, picturesque windows along several walls. Large thick leather furniture sat positioned around for maximum comfort. He shot a look at Elijah.

"It's your call," Elijah said since this was his mission.

River tipped his head. "Bravo team?" he whispered.

"I have eyes on the room," Isaac said. "There are five targets. I repeat, five targets."

"Alpha team, this is Charlie team. We also have eyes on the targets," Oliver responded.

"You put a bullet in anyone's head if they so much as look twitchy," River ordered his men.

"Roger that," Oliver replied and Isaac echoed.

With the familiar rush of his adrenaline, the tension thickened and River slowly stepped out, gun hand out-stretched, one hand supporting the other. He quickly darted a look left and then right, never moving his gun from the suspects in front of him.

His gaze landed on the man in the middle of the group.

Gillman Berk, whom he vaguely remembered, was all grown up. They'd attended the same high school, but Gillman had been two years behind him. On both sides of the man stood four big, beefy men. Hard ass types, gang tattoos, hired guns, thugs, dressed in bulky leather jackets carrying more firepower than brains.

Gillman standing in the middle was far from calm. Sweat dripped from his upper lip and brow. The gun Gillman held shook in his hand and was pointed down at the floor. The guy's finger wasn't even on the trigger. River frowned.

Elijah and Maddox slowly inched forward, guns trained on the beefy men. Of Dillon there was no sign, but he didn't doubt the man was slipping around to flank the enemy.

Gillman looked nervous more so than a guy with leverage should be. All the men held guns. The man to Gillman's right had his gun pointed sideways, sort of at Gillman, while the other three had their guns pointed at them.

Taking in the gun's angle, he lifted his eyes to Gillman's and saw the man's mouth tremble. River squinted. Gillman shook and the man swallowed.

Something wasn't fucking right.

Elijah's head gave a slight tip toward Gillman and River agreed with the silent acknowledgement. Gillman didn't look like a hardened criminal, but the guy holding the gun aimed at the man clearly was.

River's finger tightened on the trigger and he put a bullet in the head of the gunman who held a gun on Gillman. The gunman toppled back, gun dropping harmlessly to the floor.

"Get down!" he yelled at Gillman.

His team dove for cover behind a large recliner and

thick leather couch. The three remaining gunmen leaped for protection behind the built-in bar and starting shooting.

Gillman stumbled and a bullet caught the man and spun him around.

Maddox and Elijah popped up and returned fire while he dove for Gillman.

River grabbed the guy around the collar of his shirt and jerked him forward. He shoved Gillman back the way he'd come and spun back, firing off a few rounds before diving for cover behind a leather sofa. Bullets cleaved into the material with a thud.

Gillman landed on his ass on the carpet behind the couch, eyes wide with shock. River crouched, ripped the bottom of the guy's shirt off, and waded it up to press against the shoulder wound. He lifted Gillman's hand and pressed it hard.

"Keep the pressure on and stay down!" he barked at the guy.

River popped up and saw Dillon flying through the air. The guy literally skated down the length of the bar and fired two times, taking out one of the perps. For such a big guy, Dillon could fucking fly.

One thug dodged out from the end of the bar, returning fire. Both Maddox and Elijah quickly dispatched the man.

Dillon slammed an elbow into a criminal's face and then shoved the guy to the floor where he zip-tied the man's hands and feet.

Gunfire outside erupted and Dillon spun, running for the patio door off of the kitchen. Elijah and Maddox sprinted after Dillon.

River spun and stalked to the couch to gaze down at Gillman. The man had gotten sick. Thrown up on the carpet.

River reached down and gently helped him stand, checking the shoulder wound. The man's light blue eyes were scared and wide.

Fucking hell.

What the ever living fuck was going on?

∞

Maddox

He dodged out of the side door after Dillon and felt Elijah take up his flank.

The house was built into the earth and in front of them lay a circular, three level, metal stairwell that he assumed took them up and out onto the grounds. The gunman leaped up the metal stairs, spun, and fired. Bullets pinged loudly and ricocheted off the metal railing, flying in several different directions.

"Cover me," he said and leaped to the end of the stairs and ran up them.

Elijah aimed and shot upward along with Dillon, allowing Maddox to reach the first level of the stairwell, dodging bullets as he went.

"Wait for the reload," Maddox said, and when the bullets stopped, he yelled, "Now."

Maddox lifted and fired several more rounds. Both Elijah and Dillon dodged up the stairs after him and hunkered by his side.

"This is Alpha team," Elijah said into the comm. "We're pinned down in the southwest stairwell, first level."

"Charlie team, copy. We are too far away," Oliver said. "Bravo, what is your position?"

"Clearing a path from the west side of the building," Isaac said. "Will be there as soon as possible, Captain."

"Someone come take this fucker out," Elijah growled, firing upward.

Both Elijah and Dillon provided him more cover fire, so Maddox pushed up the remaining stairs of the second level, shooting at what he could see of the gunman. Both Elijah and Dillon shot at the guy. Maddox reloaded his weapon.

Suddenly, a scuffle sounded, muffled gunfire, and then silence.

"Bravo team has arrived," Isaac sang cockily into the mic. Tipping his head back, Maddox smirked upward to find the Infinity soldier grinning down at them.

"Casualties?" Elijah barked into the mic.

All teams confirmed there were four fatalities and several gunmen zip-tied and gagged.

Elijah called it clear when all teams verified each area of the estate was secure.

Returning to the house, he spotted River at the kitchen counter handing Gillman Berk a glass of juice from the refrigerator.

"It went through. Bleeding's stopped. Stitches should hold." Oliver, Infinity's medic, tended the guy's shoulder wound, gave the guy a shot with a needle, then packed up his gear and stepped back.

Gillman didn't look like a hardened criminal nor a drug lord. In fact, the guy looked innocent and scared.

"What the hell is going on?" he said, stepping further into the room.

Gillman jerked and the juice almost spilled, but River reached out and steadied the glass.

River tossed him an impatient look. Elijah, Isaac, and Dillon stepped through the door. The rest of the team came in by way of other entries.

"Guys, this is Gillman Berk, and he has a story to tell," River said and gave Gillman a gentle nod.

The guy who looked to be a bit younger than River took a long, shaky breath.

"I never took Triton. I don't do drugs and I'm not a dealer… like my old man was."

"Start from the beginning," Elijah said gently.

"My father was the drug dealer. When he died, I swore I would put an end to it. I managed it for a few months and then Rutherford Boyd showed up."

"Rutherford Boyd?" he asked.

"He's a drug dealer and gun runner that operates out of Austin. He said I was to keep my father's agreement with him or he'd kill my baby sister." Gillman gulped. "She's in college south of here in San Antonio. He sent me a video of her walking around campus with her friends."

"Base? You getting this?" River said.

"Rutherford Boyd. I'm on it," Sam replied.

"Why didn't you contact the police and have her picked up?" Maddox asked.

"Because in the video, she's walking with her boyfriend."

"And?" He frowned.

"Her boyfriend works for Boyd."

"Damn it," he growled. "That means they can get to her before the cops."

"Yeah." Gillman swallowed hard. "I hope you got all of his men who were here, because if you didn't, they'll call him and she'll be dead."

"How many men did he have here?" River asked Gillman.

"Thirteen."

River lifted a hand and gave a circle motion to the team. "Canvas the area. I want every one of Boyd's men accounted for."

Infinity scattered out the front, side, and back of the house.

"We're sending an expert team to pick up your sister and keep her safe," River told Gillman.

"Where is Triton?" Maddox asked the guy.

"Boyd took him."

Maddox's blood ran cold, then hot, and his fists clenched.

"He's waiting for one of his men to drive the truck to their location and then he said he'd release Triton, but I know he won't," Gillman hiccupped.

"All perpetrators are accounted for," Isaac said over the mic.

He grabbed a jacket off the back of a nearby chair and draped it over the man's shivering form. Gillman gave him a grateful look and buried his face in the coat.

"Gillman?" Maddox waited for the young man to lift his head. "Do you know where the trade location is?"

"Yes."

CHAPTER THIRTEEN

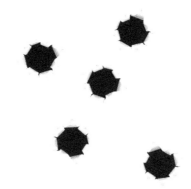

River

SEVERAL MINUTES LATER, DILLON STEPPED BACK THROUGH the door with a gun on one of the gunmen. The guy hesitated when he noticed the group.

"You fucking talk and your sister is dead!" the man growled and Dillon slapped the guy on the back of the head and shoved him forward.

Maddox lunged, gripped the man's shirt, and lifted his gun. The man's eyes grew wide and zip-tied hands came up to ward off Maddox.

Stunned at Maddox's loss of control, River froze for a split second and then leaped across the distance and set his hand on Maddox's rippling forearm.

"Hey," he whispered quietly, his heart pounding, "we might need him." Maddox drew in a deep breath before releasing the guy with a hard shove into the wall.

River dropped his hand and then jerked his head at Dillon, who took the culprit into another room.

"Gillman?" River said.

"Yes," the man's voice wobbled.

"When and where are you supposed to take the truck to Boyd?"

"Tomorrow afternoon. He'll be at the old ghost town," Gillman said, naming a location east of them along a local highway.

"Okay. Tell me everything about where your sister is located."

With a shaky voice, Gillman filled them in.

"Base? You got that?" River said.

"Roger," Sam said. "Sending a team for retrieval of Gillman's sister."

Dillon reentered the room and took up a spot near the bullet riddled couch, arms crossed against a massive chest, muscles rippling. "He's tied up," the weapons specialist said.

Gillman threw the big man a nervous glance.

"Now, we wait," River told Gillman, trying to soften his voice.

"Alpha team?" Sam said. "I have the intel on Boyd."

"Go ahead, base," River said.

"Rutherford Boyd is a major player in illegal drugs and arms dealing in Austin. He's affiliated with the drug cartel that comes in and out of Texas from Mexico."

It took two hours for a team to arrive at Gillman's sister's school. Delta team was dressed as college students and scouring the campus and her dorm. Through the small video feed attached to the front of the Delta team leader's sweatshirt, they could view the men advancing through the school.

River stood at the counter eating a sandwich Gillman had set out fixings for. Eating over the sink, he watched the video feed.

Maddox approached and leaned next to him against the counter, watching the feed as well.

"I checked in with Bull," the man said quietly after a few minutes.

"All okay?" He shoved the last bite into his mouth. He'd called Jim himself earlier, but had yet to speak to Bull. He wasn't quite sure what he'd say to his grandfather at this point.

"Yeah. Jim has every ranch hand with a loaded rifle."

"That's good, some of those men are excellent marksmen," he said.

Maddox grunted, eyes glued to the video.

"I'm surprised you even bother with Bull."

Maddox's head snapped up and the man frowned. "He may have screwed up, but Bull is family."

He searched Maddox's eyes, the blue attempting to suck him into the swirling depths. Offering promises that weren't true. It took a moment before River was able to turn to the sink and wash his hands. Hearing Maddox call Bull family made his chest ache. Once, a long time ago, they'd also been family.

"What a messed up situation," Maddox said quietly, glancing toward the kitchen door and Gillman beyond, pacing back and forth in the living room.

"Yeah, I feel for the guy," he returned, studying the paper towel in his hands.

"Infinity, this is Delta, we've retrieved Jessica Berk."

River jerked his eyes back to the video. He'd been so caught up with Maddox that he'd completely missed the retrieval.

"Roger that," River said, voice calm, getting back down to business.

"They've got her." He turned, looking at Gillman.

The man burst into tears and Oliver guided the guy over to sit on the sofa.

"Now we get Triton," River said to Maddox, careful to keep his eyes on his men.

∞

Maddox

As he stood in Gillman's massive dining room looking over the map, he knew it would be a setup.

Walking into the old town during daylight could be signing their death warrants, but Elijah and River had a plan, a damned good one too.

He gave a sidelong glance at River. The man had his head bent. Dark hair fell over his forehead. He hadn't been able to decipher River's expression earlier while standing at the sink.

Maddox found his gaze suddenly roaming over every inch of muscle displayed beneath the tight, gray t-shirt. The man's arms were tattooed in intricate black designs that sleeved down both and he wanted to see them all.

"There's one main entrance into the town." Elijah pointed to a printout Gillman had supplied of the area.

Maddox tore his gaze away from River and back to the task at hand.

"There are several outbuildings. It used to be a small mining town from what I can find," River murmured.

"It was," Gillman said.

"We position people here, here, and here." Elijah pointed to the backs of two buildings and the top of one.

"I suspect they'll have Triton inside one of the buildings," Blade said.

"No, they won't," he disagreed, and they all looked at him. "They'll use the mine," he told them.

"There's an open mine there?" Isaac asked, eyebrows raised.

"Open enough," Maddox said.

"Maddox is right," River said. "They'll put Triton in the mine, if they're smart, and make us go in and get him."

"Which means they can get away with the truck while you're inside," Gillman said.

"We won't all be inside," Elijah assured the man.

"Only a few will go in. Me, Maddox, and another volunteer." River held his stare with a suddenly intense look. The man's eyes were guarded, yes, but this time, Maddox detected something else in the brown depths.

"I'll go," Diesel said.

"All right," River said to Diesel and him. "Make sure you both know what you're taking on."

"I know what I'm taking on," Maddox told the man.

"Same," Diesel growled.

"There's a chance when we get in that mine we may not be coming out," River said, looking right at him and then over at Diesel. "My guess is they'll blow it the minute we're inside," River tagged on.

"Make sure we have gear equipped for a cave in." River's eyes swung back to him.

"That town is right at the edge of my property," Gillman said. "I have mining gear. Based on this old map, I can also tell you the best place to hunker down if there is a cave in." Gillman pulled up the map of the inside of the mine on a laptop and pointed. "The main tunnel branches off into two smaller tunnels. If you are caught in the main tunnel, get to the area located after the ladder that leads down and stay there. If you're caught in one of the two smaller tunnels, there is a built in steel alcove in each one that you need to get to. It might hold until we can retrieve you."

"Do you have drilling equipment?" Maddox asked.

"Yes."

"Good," he said. "So does the Triple R."

"All right. That's it for now," River said. "Get some rest." The man strode out of the room.

Maddox was slower to follow. Walking into the other room, a den area where the television was running, a few of the guys sat watching the TV. The weather man gave an update on more heat coming with the occasional late spring showers. He sank into the large chair that sat off to the side of the large living room. Two of Infinity's men crashed on the couch.

He pulled out his phone and fired off a text to Spencer. He still had a mission to complete once their informant surfaced.

It was hard to believe they'd only been hunting Triton for two full days.

All he needed to do was get Triton back, make sure the drugs got to the authorities, and get Bull's promise to never do this shit again.

He searched for River and spotted the man stretched on the floor across the room, using his jacket for a pillow.

River was ignoring him, ignoring their connection, and as much as it killed him, Maddox thought about giving up. If he did, he could keep his secret and not feel guilty and River could continue hating him.

And for the first time ever, he gave serious thought to selling his half of the ranch.

The phone buzzing woke him up, and by the time he dug it out from the side of the chair, the call had gone to voicemail. Rubbing a hand over his face, he pushed the recliner into an upright position and rolled to his feet before walking out the back door and a few feet out into the yard.

Dialing the number that had been calling him for the last few hours, he waited.

"What the hell! Not calling me when your cousin goes missing?" Captain Spencer Turner yelled.

"I was gonna call earlier," he sighed into the phone.

"Yeah, okay. Fucker," his best friend said in a growly voice that would have made him smile if the circumstances weren't so dire.

"Truly, with the shit going on."

"I know. I was informed."

"By who?"

"You know the major can't keep shit from me. Especially when my best friend goes missing."

"Yeah. I know."

"So, talk to me."

"I got a call from my little cousin," Maddox said and filled his friend in on everything. Including the kidnapping.

"Son of a bitch. I'm so sorry, bro."

Maddox closed his eyes. "Thanks."

"Your text was kind of vague. Someone's helping you? You said River brought a team?"

"Yeah."

"Enlighten me."

"Can't."

"Oh." Spencer was quiet. "Gotcha, not over the air waves."

"Yup. I'll fill you in when I see you."

"Say no more. So your man, River?" Spencer said quietly.

"Yeah, except he isn't mine."

"Bullshit. If the guy has half a brain, then he'll still be in love with you."

"So speaks the biased best friend." He sighed. Spencer had been there during one of the darkest times in his life.

"Hey, don't cut yourself down."

The silence grew between them.

"Look, I need to get back. You want me out there?" Spencer asked.

"If you could get away."

"Just tell me if Liam Cobalt is out there," Spencer said after a long moment.

Maddox wasn't surprised Spencer had guessed the unit River was with. After all, they were all in the army.

"No, he's not. So you—"

"Okay, I'll try my best to get out there." Before he could question his friend about Colonel Liam Cobalt, Spencer cut him off.

He stood for a long time after the phone call had ended. Spencer had been there for him, been there through all the shit he'd endured. The man had listened and like the good friend he was, he told him to quit fucking whining. A noise drew his head up. He found River standing in the doorway.

He held the man's searching gaze for a long time. Words from eight years ago rang in his ears, making his chest tighten and hurt like hell.

"Mad! I'll be leaving on the ten o'clock train." River's voice had wobbled, thick with tears. "I'll wait until then. If you don't show up, I'll know you really don't love me."

Taking a slow, deep breath, Maddox turned and walked away.

CHAPTER FOURTEEN

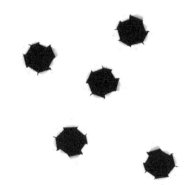

River

MADDOX HAD AVOIDED HIM LAST NIGHT, LEAVING HIM wondering who the guy had been talking to on the phone.

He downshifted the truck and parked it shy of the old ghost town. The truck's air brakes hissed and he turned the truck off and jumped from the cab. Diesel jumped from the passenger seat. A pickup pulled in behind them with Oliver at the wheel.

Pia and Blade jumped out of the pickup and headed to the back of the truck.

River went around and opened the back to let Maddox jump out of the back and the girls jumped in. River left the door slightly ajar.

The criminals would want to inspect the truck and make sure the stash was still there. They'd get more than they'd bargained for.

He turned with Maddox and Diesel and walked to one of the main buildings. Once there, he pulled his gun and headed toward the center of town.

Ahead, a man stepped out of one of the buildings. Three men came from the building to his right and two from his left and flanked the leader. The man's gaze roamed over all of their full tactical gear and weapons.

"Stop right there," the leader said, jiggling the handgun in his hand. The others lifted their guns.

River stopped, as did Maddox and Diesel beside him.

"You the cops?" the leader asked.

"No," Maddox growled.

The leader's eyes snapped to the heavily armed soldier.

"Where's the boy?" River called out across the distance.

"In the mine." The ring leader jerked his head toward the dark, gaping hole still giving Maddox a nervous look.

"Where's your boss?" Maddox called out.

"He's not here. I'm in charge." The leader spat into the dirt and then wiped his mouth. "Go get your boy in there and we'll be taking the truck."

From one of the outbuildings, he spotted Isaac and Oliver with assault rifles aimed at their targets. Dillon was lying flat on the top of the old feed store with a sniper rifle.

"Let me talk to Triton. I'm not giving you shit until I know he's still alive," River said, holding the criminal's shifty gaze.

The ring leader squinted at him and after a moment, the guy turned to the man on his right and held out a two-way radio. "Take this to the hostage and make him say something."

"What? I ain't fucking going in there!" the guy spat and

backed away. The ring leader backhanded the guy and then shot him dead. The leader held the radio out to the man on his left.

"Go," the man snarled and this time, his order was obeyed. The man snatched the radio and disappeared into the mine. Several long minutes later, they heard a crackling on the radio.

"Say something!" the man hissed through the radio.

"Maddox! Stay out, there's explosives!" It was Triton. There was a cry and then crackling silence.

Maddox took a step forward, River fisted the back of the man's vest.

"That's it," the leader said and then dropped the two-way and crushed it beneath his boot.

The gunman came jogging out from the mine several minutes later and approached them with the other radio in his hand.

River gave the signal by way of scratching his chin. He, Maddox, and Diesel dove for cover and his team opened fire.

The four men standing before him were dropped without a second's hesitation. His team fired with high powered assault rifles.

Each thug went down except for the one in the middle. The ring leader, they left alive. The guy had lost his gun, dropped flat, hands over his head and was curled into a fetal position.

Gunfire broke out in one of the buildings to his right and his team rushed to assist.

River strode forward and kicked the gun out of the ring leader's reach and then reached down to lift the guy by the back of his shirt and spin him around.

"Where are the explosives in the mine?" he snarled, holding his gun beneath the man's chin, forcing his head back.

"Inside, five hundred feet." The man's voice shook and River released the guy. Diesel held a gun on the guy.

Isaac rolled up in a small pickup loaded with mining gear. The unit converged on the pickup.

River slipped on a small air tank, hooked a water jug at his hip, and then pulled on a lightweight protection vest and a helmet with a lamp on the front.

"River." Elijah stepped up and helped him with the gear. "You good?"

"Yeah, Captain. I'll be right back," he said and pulled the rubber strap of the air mask around his neck, letting the breathing cup hang down, and slipped on a backpack filled with necessary items. Maddox and Diesel were dressed similar.

River spun and jerked the leader around and shoved him toward the wide opening. The guy staggered, righted himself, and stumbled forward.

They reached the opening and the man hesitated. He reached out and shoved the guy forward into the dark, gaping mouth of the mine.

It was wide enough to fit a truck through if needed, but they were going on foot.

With the leader leading the way, he stepped in after the guy, Maddox on his six and Diesel taking up the rear.

River turned to look over his shoulder. At the entrance stood the rest of Infinity. He gave a thumbs up and Elijah gave a nod. Oliver lifted his hand, his friend's face worried as were the rest.

He adjusted the pack on his back, turned, and headed deeper into the cave.

Flicking on the light of his helmet, he moved into the increasing darkness with the gang's leader reluctantly leading the way.

"It's up ahead," the guy's voice shook.

"Why are you nervous?" River snapped at the guy.

"Because it's set to blow."

"When?"

"Any second."

"What the fuck?" Diesel growled and shouldered past them.

"Diesel!" he shouted, but the big guy didn't listen as he jogged down the mine shaft before disappearing from view.

"Take us to where the explosives are now!" Maddox snarled and the leader stumbled forward.

A small alcove about five hundred feet into the mine came into view and the explosives were there.

River shucked off his pack, withdrew some items, and studied the timer.

Seven minutes and ticking.

"You guys are idiots. Seven minutes? I can defuse this in one," he snapped and set about defusing the bomb. It took two, but who was counting.

"Diesel?" River called out, lifting his radio.

"I'm in…"Diesel's voice came over the radio, but then a crackling sound.

"Shit. I'm going to kick his ass," he growled.

"Can we get out of here?" the leader asked, looking nervous.

"No," Maddox said, stepping up closer and watching the man. "Not until we get my cousin."

"We're going to stay here for a while. Why?" River inquired. The guy's eyes darted around.

"We need to leave!"

"Because?" Maddox asked.

"Why? You motherfucker!" he snarled and shoved the guy back against the dirt wall.

"There's more charges!" the guy cried out.

"Fuck!" He grabbed the guy and shoved him further into the mine and well past the five hundred feet mark. They came upon a ladder that would take them lower into the mine. Jumping down, they came up to the second device.

The timer said four minutes. He defused this one in one minute and wiped away the sweat gathering on his forehead before replacing his helmet.

They were in the large area Gillman had pointed out as a safe spot, with two tunnels branching out on the far side of the space.

Maddox shoved the leader farther across the open space. The guy was blubbering now.

"Diesel?" River tried the radio again.

A crackle was his only answer.

They walked a few more feet when an explosion came from deeper in the mine. One of the small tunnels caved in as they watched.

The ceiling shook and dust trails of dirt sprinkled down on them. His heart lurched hard and he put a hand out to steady himself, keeping an eye on Maddox.

The ring leader turned and shoved past them and ran

back the way they'd come. Maddox lifted his gun as if to shoot the man, but the ceiling gave way. A bolder twice the size of a man fell on top of the thug, crushing him beneath. Chunks of earth and large rock fell, crashing to the ground.

"Run!" River shouted and shoved Maddox faster across the large area. Dread made his limbs feel clumsy, rocks showered them and all River could do was watch Maddox's back and hope like a motherfucker nothing took the man down. He couldn't remember ever praying so hard.

∞

Maddox

He fucking ran. Together, they dodged falling debris until they reached the opposite side where the two smaller tunnels branched out. One was already collapsed, but the other was open. River sprinted into it.

"No! River!" Maddox heard the high pitch of fear in his own voice and ran like hell after the man.

"Triton and Diesel might be in here!" River yelled back.

Another rumble shook the ground, bringing River to a halt. Maddox reached the man and grabbed the strap on River's tank with a sweating hand. It was a good thing because the rock and dirt over their heads gave way. The fissure opened along the wall and then another loud crack. Rocks and debris spewed outward and into the tunnel.

Maddox yanked River back and turned him around and shoved him hard. The man was nimble and leaped instead of tumbled. River spun, eyes wide, and Maddox ran toward him.

Praying.

"Run, fucking run!" River screamed at something behind him before River spun and ran back toward the bigger area.

Maddox leaped, covering the distance, and flew out of the small tunnel as rocks collapsed behind him.

The blast sent him forward to his stomach and he covered the back of his neck with his hands.

"Mad! Mad!" River's voice shouted. The man scrambled to him and brushed the debris and dust off. Fingers unclipped his helmet and then combed through his hair, searching, stroking, touching, and he groaned beneath the frantic touch.

"Fuck! Oh fuck!" River's voice cracked. Maddox laid there letting the man's hands brush over him.

He finally rolled over and blinked up. "I'm okay."

River blinked down at him and then frowned. "Well, why the hell didn't you say so?" The man scrambled back and jerked to his feet to stalk away toward the main entrance and cave-in that blocked the way out.

Maddox sat up. The light from his helmet lit up the area in front of him and River, who stood rigid and angry near the cave-in.

"Were you worried?"

"Fuck off," River snapped and pulled out a small, thin metal rod that he unfolded and snapped into place until it was a long, thin pole. Slowly, the man checked the depth of the cave-in, looking for gaps.

Maddox gently checked his arms and legs and then let out a low hiss.

"Where are you hurt?" River growled, his head snapped

up and he realized River had stopped poking the cave-in and was glaring at him.

He shook his head, but River threw the pole down and marched back over.

"I said -"

Maddox took ahold of River's arm and pulled the guy until he was leaning over him.

"Will you stop for a minute? You go poking shit and it might cave in more." Maddox looked up into River's face. Their faces were maybe a foot apart. Why was it that every time he looked into River's wide, deep brown eyes he felt as if the world fell away and every fucking thing that was wrong was suddenly right? He tried, oh how he tried to ignore the way the man's eyes dropped to his mouth, but he couldn't. River closed his eyes, cutting the hold on him and after a long moment, Maddox released River's arm. River gave a heavy sigh and dropped to his ass next to him and took a deep breath.

"I wasn't thinking. You scared the shit out of me," River complained.

"Me too," he admitted and dropped into silence.

River drew one of the electric safety lamps from his pack and turned it on. Then the man dug for the one Maddox used and turned that one on. It lit up the inside of the cave and gave Maddox the opportunity to roam his eyes over River's dusty profile. The man's hair had a layer of dust making the curly, dark strands on top appear lighter.

"Thank you," River jerked his head toward the smaller cave-in. "For yanking me out of the way."

"Anytime."

"Fuck. I hope Diesel got to Triton," he said. They'd sat there for the past hour listening to the cave-in settle into silence broken only by the occasional loose rock tumbling.

"I bet he did." River nodded and moved to stand. "I'm sure he also made it to one of the metal alcoves."

Maddox took a few sips of water, then capped the container and put it away. Shrugging off his vest, he shook it out and used it for a pillow. Fuck, he hoped River was right.

The quiet was so absolute, he turned his head to find River's dark eyes pinned on him.

"What?" he asked quietly beneath the man's searching gaze. His heart pounded.

"We might be here a long time," River began.

He drew in a deep breath and blew it out. "Maybe," he said warily.

"I think we should talk."

His eyes snapped to River. Was this his chance? Was this where he asked for River's forgiveness? His mouth opened and then closed when the words dried up. His breath stuttered when he sucked in air.

"If you can get the words out…" the man said softly.

He closed his eyes and then opened them. Took a breath, opened his mouth, then closed it. Took another breath and said the only thing his brain could come up with. "I still come home every summer."

"Why?"

"To wait for you," Maddox said simply.

River squinted at him. "I don't believe you."

"It's true."

"Why'd you end it with me if you were going to come back every summer to wait for me!" River said in disbelief.

"Back then, I had to end it." He struggled to get his words out, careful not to say too much.

"Bullshit," River said. "You were doing one more tour. I was going away to college and we were going to be together!"

"I remember." He nodded slowly, keeping his gaze on the cave wall. Rubbing his sweating hands on his pants, he fought the sudden nausea.

"We made plans for all that. You said you loved me, and then you took it back like it all meant nothing."

Maddox swallowed, and stared at River.

Everything they'd planned rolled through his head. Maddox remained still.

"So, what happened?" River asked, and the man's beautiful face creased with confusion.

"I made a mistake. But I thought when you came home the next summer we could start again, only summer never came." He briefly closed his eyes.

"What mistake?" River suddenly hissed into the silence. "And I want to know why you said you didn't love me."

His eyes snapped open. River's brown eyes filled with pain were locked on him.

"It was for the best back then." *Jesus Christ, how lame could he sound?*

"For the best?" River threw up his hands. "For whom? Were you cheating on me? Is that it? Was there someone waiting back at the base?" River threw the words like they were daggers.

"No!" He jerked back, stunned that River would think him a cheat. "No, nothing like that."

He shoved to his feet and walked back toward where

the entrance used to be, and then spun and faced River across the distance.

"I know that John Stone abused you."

Maddox froze, the words punching him. He couldn't think. *Shit. Shit.* A hot wash of heat swept up his neck and into his face. Sour welled from his stomach and into his throat and he turned to spit on the ground. He thrust both hands through his hair as the silence stretched painfully.

"You knew and you never said a word?" He croaked, finally turning to look at River.

River jerked to his feet and walked away from him. But there was only so far either one of them could go.

Fuck! Maddox fisted his hands at his sides and glanced around. There was no way out, they were stuck here together.

He set his head against the cold stone wall and took several deep breaths. "How long have you known?"

"Since I was eleven."

CHAPTER FIFTEEN

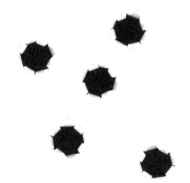

Maddox

THROUGH A FOG, HE HEARD RIVER'S VOICE.

"I overheard Andrew and Bull talking about it one day after you left with your mother," the man said quietly.

He would have been sixteen, he numbly thought. The year when the beatings became unbearable. Which was saying something because he'd been used to them since he was ten years old when his mother had left his father due to spousal abuse. Maddox got the raw end of the deal with a judge, a guy who had gone to school with his father, had ruled his mother's leaving was abandonment and gave John Stone full custody of him. He'd ended up living with his father in a rundown house on the outskirts of town.

It wasn't long after he'd been taken from his mother that John turned his anger on him. Maddox's only escape had been every other weekend with his mom until his grandfather, Andrew Stone, bought half of the Triple R. Then, at

Andrew's request, John would drop him at the ranch along with threats.

"You keep your mouth shut, boy. You hear me?" John would snarl and make him wear long sleeved shirts or lie about the bruises. "If you don't, I'll never let you visit them again."

"I...I...I...won't," he'd stammered, feeling the urge to pee or vomit, he wasn't sure which one. One thing was for sure, though, he got really good at lying and never told a living soul.

At the age of fourteen, being at the ranch was some of the best times in his young life.

His mother cried every time she had to drop him back at John's house. She never stopped trying to get full custody, but it would take her six long years before he was saved. For six long fucking years, his mother fought the judge and the courts. Nothing happened until the day his mother had gone to Andrew Stone.

"Maddox, your mother has told me some disturbing news." Andrew's kind gaze looked him over. The man reached and took his hand even though he tried to pull away.

"It's okay, honey." His mother broke down in tears. She pointed at his shirt. With terror, he saw his old and torn t-shirt had slipped and the red welts and bruises were visible at his collar bone and throat. He sobbed when Andrew gently removed his shirt.

His grandfather, a prominent figure in the community, rocked the courts in a way the town had never seen before. Not only had his mother won custody, but Andrew threatened to disown his only son if he ever abused him again. With his mother awarded sole custody, Maddox had finally been free of John Stone, or so he'd thought, at the age of sixteen.

Andrew had put an unemployed John to work on the ranch, but before he did, Andrew had the graciousness to ask Maddox first. His grandfather was a firm believer that idle hands got into trouble. Maddox had agreed because he didn't plan on going back to the ranch ever again if John was there. But time passed and he missed his grandfather.

The next time Maddox felt comfortable enough to return to the Triple R to visit Andrew and say hello to River, he'd been on a brief military leave.

He'd run into John Stone. The asshole picked up the verbal abuse as if he were a young boy but never used his fists on him again. Maddox was sure it was partly because of Andrew's warning and partly because the man didn't want to take him on physically. At the age of twenty-one, Maddox had grown tall and hard with muscle.

He'd been riding the ranch that day when he'd gotten his first look at a sixteen year old River. Maddox had booked it out of there and hadn't returned to the ranch for two more years. River had been eighteen the next time he'd come back.

That time, he'd spent the whole summer.

A boot crunched nearby and the cave came into focus. River studied him with those large, dark eyes, making him think that all things were possible.

"I should have said something," River whispered, and then looked away before looking back. "I remembered always seeing you with bruises when we went swimming." River's soft words drew his gaze.

He'd only gone in the swimming hole at dusk because he'd believed the dark hid the bruises.

"You told me you got them fighting the other boys," River doggedly continued.

"I didn't," he whispered.

∞

River

Maddox avoided his searching look and River's chest ached from the remote expression on the man's face.

"We should probably clear some of these rocks," he said, blowing out a breath.

"Yeah," Maddox replied a bit warily.

"That way when they come through it'll be clear," he said, changing the subject, giving them both a bit of breathing room.

Maddox nodded and began clearing the rocks from the floor in front of the cave-in, making a pile to the side.

River half smiled. Being with Maddox over the past few days had reminded him of their summers together. Wasn't it ironic that he was now trapped with the man he'd taken great pains to avoid for the last eight years? Wasn't it equally ironic that he no longer wanted to avoid the man?

Yet, he was still no closer to getting answers.

Maddox's reaction told River what he'd suspected for a long time, John Stone had something to do with their breakup, but River couldn't confirm it because Maddox wasn't talking.

After most of the rocks were clear, River returned to his pack and opened up a power bar to munch on.

Maddox approached at a slower pace. The man reached his side and sat nearby.

"So…the army," Maddox said softly.

"Yeah," he drawled, glad for the opening. He wanted to keep Maddox talking.

"How long before you became Special Forces?"

"I went into Special Forces training after boot camp. They changed all that. Now they train you from the start, if you apply. You only need to make the cut," he said, making light of the intense and difficult training.

Maddox whistled. "I heard of the changes, I just never thought you'd join the Army, much less Special Forces."

He shrugged and then sent Maddox a quick look. "What about you? I thought you would have left the service by now, Captain."

"No." Maddox smirked at the title.

"Why not?"

"No reason to."

"That's crap, you have your degree and the ranch," River pointed out.

"So do you," Maddox countered.

"My grandfather is still alive." The silence was sudden and deafening. "Shit. "Sorry," he said.

"It's okay." Maddox sighed. "I still miss him."

River nodded and wadded up the power bar wrapper before pushing it back into his pack. Andrew Stone had died roughly six years ago. The man had been kind and supportive of Maddox, unlike that bastard John Stone.

"I'm sorry I didn't come home for the funeral." River wanted to make up some bullshit story about deployment, but it would have been a lie. He'd sat on his bunk during leave and got shit faced until it was too late to go home.

"You're getting old, you'll need to retire soon," River teased, trying to lighten Maddox's sad expression.

Maddox's brow furrowed. "I have a few years left in me."

River grinned at the thirty-three year old. Maddox had quite a few years left in Special Forces and more if he wanted. They had waivers for that shit now.

"I want to ask you a question and I don't want a bullshit answer."

"What?" Maddox glanced warily at him.

"Why did you really break up with me?" he pushed again, ignoring the look of pain that briefly flashed on Maddox's face.

There was a long moment of silence where River held the man's blue eyes, hope lingered on the air and then died when Maddox turned his face away.

"Because I was a coward."

The words were said so softly, River's mouth fell open. Had he heard Maddox right?

"A coward?"

Maddox sighed and snatched up his backpack, the man pulled a small axe and walked toward the main cave-in. Maddox tossed the rucksack aside and then chipped away at the rubble. After a moment, the man lifted the metal rod and poked it through the gaps in the rock.

It was like going through a brick wall to get Maddox to talk.

"Why were you a coward?" He made an impatient sound in his throat, wishing he'd packed something stronger to drink than water.

"It doesn't matter," Maddox murmured and chipped away at more rock.

"It fucking matters to me," he snapped, suddenly angrier than he could ever remember being.

"River, just leave it alone," Maddox warned.

"You *are* a coward," he accused, jumping to his feet. "You were a coward back then and you're a coward now!"

The hurt swam in Maddox's blue gaze. "Thanks," the man rasped.

"Why'd you even say that then?" He glared, squeezing his hands into fists.

"I don't know, River!" Maddox yelled, smacking at the rocks.

"Maybe because you're lying to me," he yelled right back.

"I'm sorry," the man said as if that would take away years of betrayal.

"That's not good enough! Unless you tell me why," he snapped.

"I can't. I'm sorry about that too." The man smacked the rocks again and again.

The rock Maddox hit sent a small sliver, a gap racing toward the roof. River almost stopped breathing when the ceiling opened up. Lunging to his feet, he flew at Maddox, slamming into the man's back, and covered him.

Rocks fell and showered them. One smacked him in the back of his helmet and he saw stars.

"River! River!"

Maddox called his name over and over. Not loudly, but softly, like a chant. A cool, wet cloth ran over his face and brow. His helmet lay unhooked from beneath his chin, but still protected the top of his head. He slowly opened his eyes.

In the soft glow of the electric lamps, he could see the worry in the pure blue of Maddox's warm eyes. The flicker of concern from the man that had once held his heart brought a lump to his throat.

"I'm okay," River coughed at the dust, breaking the special moment, and regret caused his eyes to burn.

Maddox sat back on his heels and stared at him silently.

River rolled to his side and slowly pushed up to sit, testing his body.

"You were out." Maddox's voice sounded strangled, drawing his eyes up quickly.

"How long?"

"Long enough for me to wet a cloth."

"So, maybe a minute?" He soothed.

"Maybe," Maddox said gruffly and flashed the light into his eyes and then took his wrist and put fingers to his pulse. If the guy was trying to take his pulse, there was going to be a problem.

"Hmmm. Pulse is really fast, but your pupils look okay."

He reached up and felt around his head. There was soreness, but no major swelling. Then he briskly ran his fingers through his hair, knocking the dust away.

When his hand fell, it landed on Maddox's arm. The muscles flexed and he gazed up into the man's face. River swallowed and licked at his dry bottom lip. He tugged on Maddox's arm to bring the man down.

"River," Maddox breathed and lowered his head the same time he lifted his face. Their mouths touched and River jolted and then groaned. His hand lifted and he sliced his fingers through Maddox's dark hair while his lips ground against the man's own, then brushed and nipped.

His other hand released Maddox's arm enough to fist the man's shirt. Maddox's lips parted, and River burrowed in, returning the heated kiss. Maddox groaned and nipped at his bottom lip. River gasped at the sting and then the kiss deepened, if that were possible. After several long minutes, he tore his mouth away, sucked in long gulps of air, and dropped his shaking hands.

"Thanks for saving me," he whispered, sounding like he had a frog stuck in his throat.

"No." Maddox shook his head. "Thank you. You keep saving me," Maddox said, sounding like he'd swallowed the same frog.

CHAPTER SIXTEEN

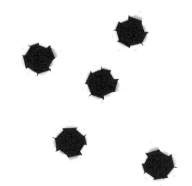

Maddox

M ADDOX SUCKED IN ANOTHER BREATH AND SHOVED TO HIS feet, trying like hell to get his dick calmed down. He brushed down the front of his pants to knock off the dust for something to do as he licked at the taste of River on his lips.

A low hum suddenly filled the cave. He spun and found River's eyes on him.

"They're drilling," the man said.

"Yeah." Rubbing at the back of his neck, Maddox took a deep breath.

River gave a small huff. "Won't be long now."

Spinning away from the temptation of River, he strode to the entrance and the growing noise. The rock vibrated against his palm.

He glanced back to see that River had shifted onto his side, pillowed his head on his arms, and closed his eyes, as if nothing had occurred between them when that kiss had rocked Maddox's world.

After several long moments, River continued ignoring him, Maddox slowly approached. Scrunching his vest into a pillow, he eased down, stretched out, and closed his eyes for one minute.

The young man stood next to the stallion and together they looked magnificent. He'd never seen anything he'd wanted more than River Seeger.

The stallion danced around the young man, then nosed in close and knocked against him while River laughed and held the apple in his hand out with a flat palm. The stallion sniffed the eighteen year old and then the apple as if deciding which he liked best.

Maddox would have gone for River. The horse chose the apple.

"You're a good boy, aren't you, Zeus," the young man crooned to the beast and Maddox swallowed hard and adjusted himself. As if sensing him there, the dark-haired man turned his head. The smile brought back the kiss they'd shared last week. Their very first kiss, but if Maddox had his way, it would not be their last.

Patting the stud, River turned and walked toward him, long legs eating the distance, and the semi Maddox's cock was sporting raced to full blown hardness. He spun and headed toward the barn.

With a laugh, River broke into a run and beat him there.

A noise woke him and he stilled, listening to the low hum of the drill growing closer.

He turned his head and found River still dozing next to him. His eyes dropped to the man's mouth, surrounded by short, dark hair in the beginning of a not-quite-there beard and mustache. He wanted to do nothing more than to reach out and grip the back of River's neck and pull him close to steal one more kiss. He needed one more kiss.

River's throat moved and tongue darted out to lick at his bottom lip. Suddenly, Maddox's eyes flickered up and found River's eyes darkened with a blazing heat.

Maddox reached out and fingered the short stubble growing on the tip of the man's chin. After a moment, he released River's chin and rolled to his feet, ignoring the sound the man made.

Heading back to where he'd stupidly hit the rock near the cave-in, he found his axe. The debris and rock had buried his pack. Uncovering the rucksack, he lifted it. The lid on the canister he'd brought for water cracked and dumped half the water on the ground.

"Damn it," he muttered, righting the container.

"It's okay, I have a full one. Between us, we should be good until they get through," River said, coming over.

The man reached for his pack and Maddox released it. River walked back over to his own pack and sat down. He followed, unable to take his eyes off the somewhat dusty man. Unzipping the pack, River pulled out the supplies within and then added his to the pile. He placed the water containers side by side.

"We should conserve, though," River said, glancing over at him when he took a seat nearby.

River sighed and laid on his back with his hands cupped behind his head and stretched out. Maddox found his eyes once again tracing the muscles down that sleek frame, the dark fan of lashes, and the curve of the man's mouth.

He coughed, stretched out nearby, and closed his eyes. River shifted about and his eyes popped open. The man turned on his side and stared at him, he could see it through his peripheral vision. His stomach tightened.

"Remember the summer of 2010?" River whispered.

Hell yes, he remembered. Maddox had taken his yearly thirty days leave all at once and had come home to spend July with River. "Which part?" He smiled.

"The fair?"

He chuckled. "Yes." He lifted his hand and spotted the tiny mark. "Still got the scar." He turned the hand to River so he could see his knuckle.

River laughed and reached for his hand, brushing fingers over the raised skin. His mouth dried up.

That day came rushing back.

He lengthened his stride to keep up with an excited River. The nineteen year old was hell bent on experiencing everything the local fair had to offer. They were also celebrating one year together as boyfriends. Maddox had spent most of his money within the first few weeks of July, but he didn't care because River was worth it. Besides, he'd be deploying in another two weeks. Of course, they wrote, Skyped, and called each other as much as possible, but it was the one month in the summer that he lived for.

River stopped at the ring toss bottle game and one of the boys standing there handed him a few rings. River tossed them and made one, laughing delightedly. The boy next to him grinned and grabbed River to plant a kiss on his mouth. River tried to jerk away, but the guy held on.

Maddox reached them in two strides, spun the guy around, and punched him in the nose and then in the mouth.

He grabbed River's hand and they ran. They reached the

parking lot before he slowed down and let River check his hand before dabbing at it with his t-shirt.

Gazing down into River's beautiful face, Maddox bent his head and removed any signs of the other man's kiss from River's lips.

"Tray had a chipped tooth for the summer, still has a crooked nose I bet," River said, bringing him back to the cave. He hadn't known at the time it was a boy River had known from school. The word spread like wildfire through the community that River had a boyfriend and from that day on, nobody tried anymore moves on River. That was worth the price of a tiny scar on his knuckles.

"Good. That's what he got for making a pass at you."

River snorted with a soft chuckle and when the man tossed him an amused grin, Maddox smiled.

CHAPTER SEVENTEEN

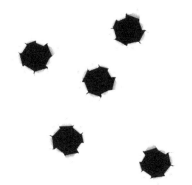

River

MADDOX'S EYES WERE FILLED WITH A WARMTH THAT HELD him riveted. The air between them grew heated and thick. The man's throat moved when he swallowed and River gritted his teeth to curb his need to take Maddox's mouth again in another kiss. Maddox's tongue darted out to lick at his lower lip and if River wasn't mistaken, the man moved a small inch closer.

A sudden muffled sound ricocheted off of the stone, cutting through the tense moment. It sounded much like a flashlight was being struck against the inside of the cave.

It struck three long tones in succession, then three more short, then three long.

"It's an S.O.S.," Maddox said roughly and jumped to his feet.

River sucked in a breath, rubbed his hands down his jeans, and hurried after Maddox to the cave-in of one of the smaller caves. The sound was coming from the other side of the rocks.

Maddox lifted his heavy duty flashlight and found a piece of stone. When the signal stopped, Maddox tapped out a reply.

Three long and three short. After a moment, came the reply.

"It's Diesel," River said with relief.

"Yeah," Maddox said and tapped out a question using International Morse Code.

Diesel answered that Triton was shaken up but unharmed. Diesel confirmed they could indeed hear the drilling.

"Thank god Diesel got to Triton. I hope their water lasts," Maddox said.

"It will." He gave a half smile. "Remember, the glass is always half full."

"Until we know otherwise," Maddox replied, returning the smile.

"Your grandfather taught us that." River huffed a short laugh.

"I remember."

His spine tingled. For a moment there, he'd thought Maddox was going to kiss him again. Would Maddox have if the pounding hadn't interrupted? Was he really ready to let Maddox back into his life after all that had happened? Even after the callous way the man had treated his love? Plus, he still had no freaking clue why.

"There's something I need to tell you," he said.

Maddox held his gaze.

"I have a boyfriend."

Shock widened Maddox's eyes. The man's nostrils flared and then a muscle ticked in the man's jaw.

"You're just now telling me?" Maddox stared at him.

"Yeah. I'm just now telling you." He spun away from the hurt filling those gorgeous blue eyes.

The rock at the entrance gave way and the drill the size of a canister punched through, leaving a gaping hole with light filtering in. He hurried across the area toward the small opening. The kiss had been unexpected, he should have said something right afterward, even if he and Cris were over when he got back. He darted a glance back. Maddox scowled at him, jaw tight.

"River?" Oliver called.

"I'm here," he said roughly.

Through the small opening, Oliver's dirt smudged smiling face appeared. "Anyone hurt?"

Hurt? No, only my heart is in danger.

"I'm fine, so is Maddox. Diesel and Triton are in another cave-in further into the cave, but Diesel signaled they're okay."

"Okay, hang tight. We'll have you out of there as soon as we clear more rock."

River glanced back and held Maddox's penetrating stare across the distance.

CHAPTER EIGHTEEN

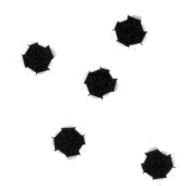

Maddox

A BOYFRIEND. RIVER WAS IN A RELATIONSHIP, BUT HAD KISSED him!

Had the kiss only been chasing the past, remembering the good times? He sighed and rubbed at his chest.

A fucking boyfriend. He ground his teeth.

Once outside, River gave orders to his men. The man was all authority. Confident in a way that heated his blood.

They stood near the cave entrance and River hadn't looked at him since leaving the dark tunnel. Maddox was going to change that soon.

When the main entrance was cleared enough to get a man through, next came the drill and jack hammer to the smaller cave entrance where Diesel and Triton were trapped.

Maddox sucked in fresh air. He guzzled down some water, then pulled on a set of work gloves and made his way back into the larger cave to help with clearing the rocks that trapped Triton and Diesel and also took a turn with the drill.

From start to finish, they'd been in there almost twelve hours.

The rocks gave and a dusty Diesel handed a slightly bruised Triton through the hole. Maddox was there to catch his young cousin, lifting him up into a tight hug and hustling him out of the cave.

Triton took in several deep breaths. He was shaking, and then got sick in the dirt.

Diesel came out looking like a piece of the mountain and covered in dirt.

Triton took one look at the big guy and ran back to throw his arms around the giant. Diesel patted Triton's back as the young man sobbed in his arms.

Maddox held Diesel's gaze over Triton's head and saw the worry there. Maddox approached and shook Diesel's hand in a tight grip.

"Thank you so much," he said.

"My pleasure," the man rumbled and gently unwrapped Triton and guided his cousin back into his arms.

Triton sniffled and clung to him. The ambulance they had called was sitting beyond the SUV and he guided his cousin toward the EMTs.

He stood silently as they checked his cousin over.

"No broken bones," one EMT said, checking Triton's rib cage.

"The bruises will heal in a few weeks. He's dehydrated." The EMT hooked Triton up to an IV drip. "I'll get some fluids into him and you can take him home from here."

Another thirty minutes and they were on their way back home. It was a silent ride back to the Triple R. The screen door opened with a crack and Bull stepped out onto the porch, his cane thumping. Triton got out and walked up to River's grandfather and hugged him tightly.

"I'm so sorry," Bull whispered brokenly into Triton's hair.

Maddox stepped up onto the porch and guided Bull and Triton into the house. River and the rest of the team followed.

An hour or so later, showered and dressed, found him sitting on the edge of his cousin's bed. Triton stood at the closet wearing faded jeans, attempting to pick out a shirt to wear. The boy was taking a long time to choose a color.

"So, you feeling okay?"

"Yeah." Triton quickly nodded and pulled on a blue shirt that made his curly black hair shine. "I won't be going into any dark places though," his cousin joked with a shaky laugh.

He smirked. "Not even with a certain man for company?"

His cousin blushed and finger combed his hair. "Maybe."

"You know that tragic circumstances sometimes make people feel connected when typically, they wouldn't," he cautioned his young cousin.

"I know," Triton sighed, lifting a towel from the floor. "Plus, I have Clay."

"One of Clay's friends was involved in all this."

"Who?" His cousin spun, eyes wide, clutching the towel to his chest.

"Damon Reding. He's dead."

"I met Damon a few times. He was into some bad shit. Clay doesn't really take me around his friends." Triton chewed his lip.

"Well, I'd appreciate it if you'd think carefully about associating with Clay," he said cautiously, because warning Triton not to do something was a good way to get Triton to do exactly the opposite.

Triton looked down at his hands for a long time.

"Hey." He frowned and when Triton looked up, Maddox said, "You know if there's anything you ever want to talk about, I'm here."

Triton smiled and walked into his arms. He hugged him tightly.

"I know."

He took the stairs down and Triton went ahead. Reaching the den, he stepped inside and found half the unit waiting.

River and Elijah were missing as well as Pia and Blade.

He walked over to the bar and poured a shot of whiskey. He turned and took a swallow.

"Help yourselves," he said to the room and a few people got up and poured a drink.

River came down the stairs looking fresh and hot in black pants, boots, and a skin-tight, short-sleeved, gray t-shirt that showed off his tattoos. The man's hair was a shiny mess, wet with water from his shower. River's dark eyes glittered when they finally held his across the distance.

He roamed his gaze down the man's trim form and then let his eyes linger on River's lips. The taste and feel came rushing back. He returned River's heated gaze. Boyfriend or no, River wanted him.

Game on, he thought and then choked on his drink when River flashed him a quick devilish smile. The move was so goddamned sexy, his heart lurched and then slammed around in his chest.

Sound on the stairs brought Elijah and then Diesel into the room and they headed toward the dining room where Frank had large plates of spaghetti and garlic bread set on the table.

They converged, taking seats and filling their plates. Some laughter and low conversation filled the room, but mostly the sound of hungry people eating.

Maddox hit his fork against his glass.

"Thank you, everyone," he said gruffly once he had everyone's attention.

"Yes!" Triton said. "Thank you." His young cousin darted a look at Diesel and ducked his head.

"Cheers," River said, and the rest of family and Infinity agreed.

Glasses were tapped together and more liquid followed.

"What's next?" Bull asked.

The room fell silent.

"We'll take care of it, grandpa," River assured Bull, but River's eyes were locked on him. A slight smile curled the man's full mouth.

Maddox returned River's small smile.

"Hey, sheriff's here," Frank said and turned from the kitchen window. Maddox pushed back from the table and headed out the front door and onto the large porch. The screen door creaked open, followed by the sound of several booted feet.

A sheriff's pickup pulled up out front and Stan Farnsworth got out and hefted up his big black belt to hitch up his pants beneath his round belly.

Maddox headed down the front steps to meet the man.

"Maddox," Stan drawled with a nod.

"Sheriff." Maddox gave a slow nod.

Stan looked around and noticed the people on the porch, mostly standing in shadows. River, arms folded, leaned against the porch post.

"River." The sheriff nodded.

"Stan." River nodded back.

Stan sniffed, hitched his pants again, and looked across at Maddox.

"Had some trouble south of town a few days ago," the sheriff drawled slowly.

"So I heard," Maddox returned just as slowly.

"Seems that the gang running things over there was tied up tighter than a Christmas tree during transport," Stan continued.

Maddox said nothing. The sheriff looked past him to River, then back to him.

"Now, the way I figure it, you boys would tell me if you had a hand in any of that now, wouldn't ya?"

"Of course, sheriff." Maddox crossed his arms and smirked.

Stan nodded. "That's what I told the mayor." Stan smirked back and turned back to his truck.

"Oh," Stan turned back one last time with fingers to the brim of his dusty cowboy hat. "You boys have a nice night."

"You too, Stan," River called from the porch.

"Take care, Sheriff," Maddox echoed.

CHAPTER NINETEEN

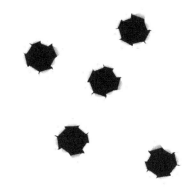

River

T HE ONLY ONES LEFT WERE HIM, MADDOX, AND THE TEAM. Bull and Triton had gone up to bed.

The table was quiet as they sat drinking coffee and looking over the plans to take out Rutherford Boyd.

Maddox, after pouring a cup of coffee, had snagged the chair directly next to him. Every so often, Maddox reached a finger to point at a section of the plans and brushed him in passing. Or it was a casual hand on his back or shoulder as he moved forward. The touches were slowly driving him crazy. When Maddox leaned again, River pushed his shoulder against the man and didn't move. Neither did Maddox. His pulse hummed and his cock thickened, making his jeans uncomfortable.

"It's a high-rise. It's going to be tricky getting in," Elijah said. "But doable."

"We'll need badge access," he murmured and let out the

breath he was holding when Maddox finally moved. It felt like a string keeping them together had suddenly snapped and released him. He didn't know whether to be happy or irritated. He adjusted himself beneath the table.

The man went for another cup of coffee and when he returned to the table, he took a seat across from him leaving River feeling oddly bereft.

A sexy as all hell smile played at the man's firm lips and River wanted to wipe it off with a kiss. Telling Maddox that he had a boyfriend hadn't done a damn bit of good to dampen River's desire for the man.

He should really come clean and tell Maddox that he and Cris were on their way out. Maybe he would once Maddox came clean about their past.

"I think I have an idea," Sam said, flipping her laptop around and showing them a face. "This is the list of employees. This guy in particular is Boyd's personal assistant and he's single."

"So you seduce him and get a copy of his key," Pia said with a grin. "I like it."

"Oh no," Sam laughed. "He's gay, so it's going to need to be one of you," the woman said, looking around at the men.

"I'm not gay," Zane said. "So count me out."

Isaac snorted and Zane shot him a dark look.

Oliver laughed and said quickly, "Of course, this is a job for me."

"Pffft," Isaac chortled. "You'd end up flirting him to death and forget about getting the badge."

"Hey!" Oliver complained, looking affronted.

"All right, calm down," Elijah ordered and the unit

looked at their leader. "I think the best man for the job is River."

"Why?" Maddox blurted out, drawing everyone's attention including his.

Elijah studied Maddox. "Because while most of the unit, if I do say so myself, are good looking, River is without a doubt the hottest."

"Depends on where you're sitting," Zane murmured with a smirk.

The room filled with chuckles and some elbowing occurred.

"I'll do it," he said.

"I'm going with you," Maddox said, giving him a dark look. Was that jealousy River spotted in the man's intense blue gaze? River's stomach fluttered.

"Okay," River agreed once he was able to form the words. "But this is my show. You stay hidden."

After a moment, Maddox gave a brief nod.

"Okay, I want Pia, Blade, and Dillon here, here, and here." Elijah pointed to several locations around Rutherford Boyd's building. "Zane and Isaac, I want you inside, so make it happen. I don't care if you're a guest or disguised as a worker, get in there and take up a position and then report back."

"Roger that," Zane said with a wink.

Isaac rolled his eyes. "Great…I get stuck with the player of the year."

"Hey!" Zane frowned.

"Kidding," Isaac smirked.

"River, get that badge. It's the easiest access to Boyd's office," Elijah said. "If you can't get that badge, we'll regroup and make a plan B."

"Copy that, sir."

"It's the weekend. Get eyes on the assistant and let me know when you find him," Elijah ordered the team.

They all agreed and filed out of the room, some heading upstairs to sleep and others went into the large living room.

He darted a glance at Maddox and licked at his suddenly dry lower lip. The dark haired man zeroed in on his tongue, then tipped his head slightly toward the back door. After a moment, Maddox stood and strode out of the room.

River held his breath and waited for what felt like a few minutes, but was only seconds before he shoved up from his chair. Palms sweating and heart pounding, he followed.

CHAPTER TWENTY

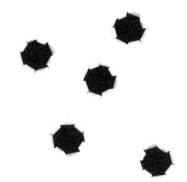

Maddox

H E STOOD OUTSIDE ON THE BACK PORCH TRYING TO GET HIS racing heart under control. He could only hope that River took the hint and came after him. The only thing that would hold the guy back was the fact that River was in a relationship. Well, that and he hadn't really told River about what had happened in the past.

If River did a no show, then Maddox decided he'd be a man about it and back off. He didn't want to break up a happy couple. But damn it, they'd kissed and also flirted hard at the table. The chemistry between them was still there and stronger than ever. He'd felt it. That had to mean something.

"Hey." The quiet voice next to him dried up every bit of spit in his mouth.

"Hey," he managed and then spun. "Walk with me," he asked, and then headed down the stairs and toward the barns that sat in the distance.

River dropped into step at his side.

The night was filled with the sounds of crickets chirping, a few birds still awake in the dark, and the low singing of cattle in the distance. Every once in a while, a horse would snort in a nearby fenced in corral.

They reached the fence and he set his arms on the top of the railing and his boot on the bottom.

"A relationship," he murmured. "You dropped a bomb on me."

"I'm sorry."

"How serious is it?" He turned his head and held River's gaze. In this area, there was enough light coming from the outside sensor and barn lights to see the man's beautiful face.

"Why?" River smirked.

"You kissed me. So I'm asking you, how serious is your relationship?" he demanded, that sexy smirk drawing him nearer.

River shook his head, hesitated, and then said, "He gave me an ultimatum. Leave my work or he was going to leave me."

"What the hell?" he growled.

River laughed, the sound jubilant and sort of relieved. "I know, right?"

"What did you tell him?"

"I told him I wouldn't do it."

"So you're *not* in a relationship."

"You'd think that would end it, right? But no. He wants me to cool down and talk when I get back." River sighed and turned toward the railing.

He moved and gripped River's arms and turned him toward him. "Call it off."

"Why?" River challenged.

"Because you kissed me," he reasoned.

"It was only a kiss."

He crowded close and the man's breathing became swift, head tilted back, lips parted.

"It was a promise," he argued and lowered his head so the words brushed against River's mouth.

"Fuck, Mad," River breathed, and then gripped his shirt to pull him down. Their lips met in a hard crush that turned soft, then nibbling, then wet when he gained entry into River's mouth. He drank in the man's taste.

The man smelled delicious. Soap and a hint of cologne or something that was all River washed over him and he groaned into the man's mouth. River's arms lifted and twined around his neck and he lifted the slighter man off his feet with arms wrapped tightly around his waist.

River eased a fraction of an inch to laugh against his lips. He smiled and lowered River to his feet.

The clouds that were threatening to break suddenly rumbled and the sky opened up, dumping rain. He snatched River's hand and laughing, he ran through the rain, pulling the man behind him until they reached the nearest barn.

They dodged inside and he tugged River to the loft ladder. Climbing upward, he reached the wide loft and walked to where the far door was open. From here, he could see forever.

River's boots made a soft sound on the floor as he drew near to where he stood.

"Our hideaway," River said and smiled up at him.

"Yeah," he smiled down.

River turned his face back to the door and gazed out over the landscape. The man was pure beauty.

Maddox took River's bicep and pulled him around, watching his eyes light up, daring for him to do something, anything.

He cupped the back of River's head and drew him closer. River reached up and wrapped his arms around his neck, pressing his body flush to his. Maddox crushed his mouth down, devouring those waiting lips.

A soft groan rose from River and his hips started grinding. Maddox drank in the kiss, tightening his grip on the man's nape. Gasping for breath, he lifted his head and tugged River to the mat that lay covered with old blankets.

River yanked at his shirt, fighting to get it up and over his head. He yanked it off and then worked at River's shirt and then the man's pants. River was stuck at getting his belt open, but then they were naked and hard and he groaned.

Pulling River down onto the mat, he dropped to his back with River sprawled on him.

"God, baby, I missed you." He tugged River's head down, fisting a hand in the hair at his nape and took his mouth in a slow, deep kiss until he felt his cock grow between them.

"Mad," River groaned, straddling his waist and undulating his hips.

He smoothed his hands down the man's muscled chest, flat stomach, and then closed his hand around the hard cock he found. River squirmed, gasped, and thrust his cock into his hand. Maddox lifted his other hand to smooth it up the man's stomach, chest, and then twisted his nipple.

River's head fell back, hips grinding his balls down.

"You're so beautiful," he groaned.

"Oh god, Mad." River leaned over and captured his lips. Tongues tangled and teeth nipped.

Reaching between them, Maddox closed his large hand around both of their cocks, locking them together, and stroked them simultaneously.

He groaned and River gasped into his mouth before lifting upward.

"Oh yeah, Mad, yes, oh fuck," River chanted, undulating and thrusting. Thrusting his dick against the inside of his hand.

"Yeah, like that, baby," he gritted out between his teeth. Pleasure split through him, tightening his balls and gut. River was grinding, panting, and thrusting.

"I'm going to come," he said, feeling the pleasure build and he wasn't sure if he could hold off.

"No!" River cried.

∞

River

"Not yet," he said gasping as he held off his own orgasm. He shoved back upright to straddle Maddox and gazed down at the man splayed out before him and smiled. River reached and roamed his hands over every inch of hard skin he found.

"Oh, baby, that's not helping," Maddox groaned.

"Do you have a condom?" River whispered, looking down into Maddox's eyes.

"In my pants," the man rasped.

River leaned over, snagged up the jeans, and searched Maddox's wallet. Not only a condom, but he also found a small packet of lube.

Maddox's blue eyes glittered. River removed the man's hand from their cocks and tore open the packet with his teeth. He slowly rolled the rubber onto Maddox's thickness.

"Fuck," Maddox hissed and his hips bucked.

He bit his bottom lip and then situated the rubber down tightly. Taking the lube, he smeared some on the tip and down the sides, lifting his eyes to hold Maddox's gaze.

"Let me use some to prepare you," Maddox husked.

"No, I'll do it." He smiled and reached around to lube up his entrance. He slipped one finger inside, but he wanted to be tight when he took Maddox's cock - so he didn't spend too much time. He wanted that bite of pain to remember when he moved about later.

Lifting up, Maddox reached down between them and then the man was at his entrance. He sucked in a breath, licked his lips, and lowered himself down on the thick, hot dick. He held the man's eyes. Maddox caught at his hips as his tight ring of muscle gave way and he sank down.

"Shhhhh fuck," Maddox groaned and, still holding his gaze, the man's fingers dug into his hips.

He hissed and lifted and then sank down. Easing forward, he kissed Maddox on the lips and ground his ass down until he was fully seated.

The impalement was slow and hot. Pain gave way to pleasure when he moved.

"I can't hold it," Maddox groaned, head tossed back, veins bulging at his neck.

River lifted up and then plunged down repeatedly.

Maddox's fingers clenched onto his ass cheeks as the man pistoned upward.

"Yeah, Mad, right there. Oh fuck, right there," he groaned and Maddox slammed home.

The orgasm raced up his spine, squeezed his balls, splashed into his gut, and he yelled with the intensity. His yell turned into a muffled sound as he convulsed. Ropes of cum spewed out of his dick and streamed across Maddox's chest. He gasped and then Maddox groaned low and long, thrusting and thrusting until the man stilled, every muscle locked, then jerked as Mad spasmed and found release.

River collapsed and Maddox held him tightly. They lay like that, gasping and panting, until they quieted. He never wanted to move from this spot. He pillowed his head on Maddox's chest and gazed toward the wide barn loft door. The rain was still going, streaming down the wood, and the opening resembled a waterfall.

He rubbed his raspy cheek against Maddox's chest before he moved and wiped them clean with the edge of one of the old blankets.

The man's eyes were closed and his face relaxed, and if River didn't know better, he'd think him sleeping.

Maddox hadn't changed all that much in the past eight years. Sure, the lines etched next to his mouth and eyes had deepened, but they gave him a mature look that River found exciting. Maddox's chest and arms had thickened with muscles as well, but every inch of the man seemed so familiar. Like picking up a beloved guitar to play after all these years.

His own changes were far greater than Maddox's. He was very different from the skinny and somewhat hesitant twenty year old that Maddox had walked away from and he wondered if Maddox liked the changes. By the way the man was looking at him and the light in his blue eyes, River was going to take that as a yes.

The breakup had done more than dented his self-esteem all those years ago. River had mourned for their lost love. He'd yearned for the man lying in his arms, and any man he'd been with after Maddox had paled in comparison. It had taken a long time, but eventually, he'd resigned himself to a life without Maddox.

Was he really contemplating another go?

Maddox gave him a crooked smile. His own lips curved with an answering grin.

"Hey there," Maddox croaked.

"Hey." He leaned down to nuzzle the man's mouth with his own and steal another kiss.

"We should get back," he whispered with regret.

"Yeah," Maddox sighed and ran his hands up the back of his thighs and up over his ass to squeeze each cheek before sliding the large, warm palms up his back.

River took another soft kiss and then sat up and rolled to his side.

"I'm starved," Maddox suddenly complained.

"You just ate," he laughed.

"River? Maddox?" Jim called.

His eyes grew wide and he scrambled for his pants. He hopped on one leg and then the other. Maddox put the pants on the ground, stepped into both legs, and then jumped to get his up in one go. River snickered trying not to laugh. They fought over the shirts on the ground. He tugged his and then broke out in laughter when Maddox put his on inside out. The man grinned and yanked his shirt off to reposition it. He sat on the edge of the makeshift bed to tug on his boots and Maddox did the same on the other side.

River, finished with his boots, leaned back against Maddox. The man tipped his head back and their heads touched and he stayed like that for a long time.

"We should go," Maddox husked.

"Yeah," he said with regret and rolled to his feet. Reaching out a hand, he pulled Maddox up before heading to the ladder and dropping down to the barn floor below.

River dusted off his pants and turned in a full circle. The barn was empty.

Maddox followed him down the ladder.

"Guess Jim got tired of waiting."

"Or figured it was better not to disturb us," Maddox growled playfully and grabbed him around the waist. He tugged free with a laugh and walked to the barn door.

The rain was still coming down hard, dripping off the edge of the door.

"Unless you want to brave getting soaked, we should probably wait it out," he murmured.

"What shall we do?" Maddox asked, coming up behind him, lips on his neck.

He turned and searched Maddox's face. "Talk."

Worry flooded Maddox's face before he looked away.

"About what happened eight years ago," River pressed.

CHAPTER TWENTY-ONE

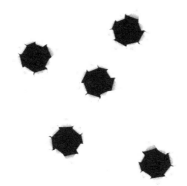

River

MADDOX WENT QUIET, LIKE HE HAD IN THE CAVE AFTER HE'D revealed knowing about the abuse. River's gut told him that John Stone had something to do with this.

The piece of shit had intimidated Maddox so much, he had hidden the fact that he was gay from his father.

River had come out at the age of sixteen. Maddox hadn't been able to. River's heart hurt for that young boy, but also for the torn man before him.

Maddox turned back to him and lifted a hand. Fingers brushed against his cheek. The man gazed at him with a light of love in his eyes. River lifted his hand and closed it over the top of Maddox's, holding the man's hand to his cheek.

"I want you to tell me what happened," River breathed. "What took you away from me."

Maddox stared at him. "It doesn't matter. All that matters is that we're together."

"Are we?" His head tipped and he narrowed his eyes, releasing his hold on Maddox. "Because I can't start a life built on secrets and lies."

Maddox opened his mouth, then closed it and swallowed before rubbing a hand over his mouth. Pain swam in the man's blue eyes and River wanted nothing more than to take Maddox into his arms and make it all better.

"You must know," River whispered. "There's nothing you could say that would make a difference to how I feel about you."

"This would." Maddox took a step away from him and River's heart lurched. "Why can't we move forward without rehashing the past?" Maddox begged.

River shook his head. "I can't."

Again, the man opened his mouth to speak, but nothing came out. They looked at each other for a long moment and then Maddox turned and walked out into the rain.

"Fuck," River whispered, releasing the breath he'd been holding, and blinked against the sting in his eyes.

∞

Maddox

Reaching the southwest barn, he grabbed and pulled on a rain slicker hanging on the wall and tugged his black cowboy hat low over his eyes. He saddled one of the stock horses and rode out into the rain.

A half an hour later, the rain had stopped, but the ground was muddy. He glanced around, he'd ended up in the north pasture.

Both he and the mare were rain soaked. He pushed her up over an incline. When she skated down the mud on the other side, he slowed with a pounding heart.

Slipping from her back, he ran his hands over her, brushing and checking her legs before he pulled her muzzle around and ran his hands over its softness.

"I'm sorry, girl," his voice broke and she nuzzled him. He leaned his forehead to her neck. She stood patiently.

He'd lost River's love. Again. And his only excuse had been he was still a coward. Like he'd told River in the cave. He was a coward because he hadn't been able to stand up to his father when it mattered the most.

"You piece of shit!" his father had said, coming into the barn. The man had come upon him right after he'd kissed River.

Thank fuck the guy hadn't actually caught them in the act, but they were still standing very close. River stared frightened at Maddox's father.

John Stone was livid.

"Run," Maddox hissed out of the side of his mouth, and thank god River turned and ran.

Maddox spun around, heart pounding, because even though he was grown and on leave home from the Army, his father still held some twisted power over him.

Oh, the guy wouldn't hit him, of that he was sure, because he would have knocked the guy into next week, but he still feared the man and he couldn't figure out why.

"Rumors are going around town. You like that faggot, boy?" his father sneered.

"No!" he'd denied, trying to go around John Stone, but the man put an arm out to stop him. Still a big man, they stood eye to eye.

"What were you two fucking doing out here?"

"We weren't doing anything," he yelled, angry all of the sudden.

"Well, it better stay that way or I'll kill him."

"What?" Maddox spun and fisted his hands into his father's shirt and slammed the man back against the side of a stall. "You fucking touch him and I'll kill you."

Stone sneered in his face. "You are soft on him, I fucking knew it! Everyone knows he's a sissy boy! You a sissy boy too?"

"No! I'm not soft on him." He thought quickly. "But he's Bull's grandson and deserves to be treated with respect."

"That punk deserves a bullet to the head."

"You leave him the fuck alone!" he snarled and released his father with a hard shove.

"You won't always be around." Stone's smile turned evil. "Aren't you leaving soon, boy?"

The mare bumped him with her nose and he lifted the reins and remounted her. Guiding her around the incline, he took a small path that would take them back to the ranch.

It was dark by the time he reached the barn. He unsaddled and brushed down the mare before feeding and putting her away for the night.

Walking along the row of stalls, he reached the foaling stall where the mare from a few days ago had given birth. Had it only been three days?

The amber colored mare watched him with large, dark eyes, the tiny foal curled up in the hay. Both mother and baby were doing fine.

He spun and leaned against the stall door, looking across at the spot near the ranch office door a few feet from him. It was this exact spot that he'd broken it off with River eight years ago.

"I don't understand why you're breaking it off, we've been inseparable for years." River's voice filled with confusion. The young man wiped at his eyes.

"You call my short visits for three summers, years?" He snorted.

"Maddox!" River said angrily. *"We've known each other since your grandfather bought into the ranch when you were fourteen. Just because we didn't start dating until I turned eighteen doesn't mean you can forget all the times we hung out before then!"*

"Look, I'm leaving soon," he said, keeping his voice hard in the face of the other man's anguish. *"This isn't going to work. I'm going back to the Army,"* he'd said harshly, hardening his heart against the big brown eyes filling with tears.

"It will work! I love you, Mad."

"This was a mistake," he said between his teeth.

"No, we are not a mistake," River gasped, wiping his sweatshirt at his nose.

"We are," he said cruelly, watching the way River's face had paled. *"You need to go onto college and forget about me."* He hardened himself.

"I can't forget about you. I love you." River cried.

"No," he said, and then he said those terrible words to River. *"I don't love you."*

He stayed hard and unyielding against River's pleading before he turned and walked away. Walked away before any more damage could be done.

It was a few hours later that Bull called him.

"River is leaving for college earlier than planned." Bull told him River had bought a train ticket for later that night.

"Good."

"I don't know what happened to break it off, son. But you're making a mistake," Bull said.

"No, trust me. I'm not," he said and hung up. He spun around and his grandfather stood there.

"You are," Andrew Stone said, shaking his head. "That boy loves you."

"Well, I don't love him," he said defiantly and turned away before he cried. Both Bull and his grandfather had always supported him. He couldn't fathom why such a good man like Andrew Stone had spawned such an abusive asshole like John. It was on the tip of his tongue to tell his grandfather that John Stone hadn't changed, but before he could get the words out, the older man engulfed him in a hug and he hung on.

One thing was for sure, though, he wasn't leaving until River was safely on that train. He left his grandfather and strode across the distance to his truck.

River caught him before he could get behind the wheel. He turned and took in River's face ravaged from tears.

"Mad! I'll be leaving on the ten o'clock train." River's voice had wobbled, thick with tears. "I'll wait until then. If you don't show up, I'll know you really don't love me."

"I won't be there," he stated harshly and turned away, clenching his hands and teeth, hiding the tear that ran down one cheek.

But he'd lied.

He had been there watching River as he stood waiting for him. He'd stayed hidden until River ran and caught the train at the last minute.

Then he'd jumped in his truck and headed back to the ranch to warn John Stone one more time.

"Good thing, boy." His father spat a wad of tobacco on the dirt. "I wouldn't want to put a bullet in his head."

Maddox swallowed hard at his father's cruelty.

"If anyone is going to get a bullet, it's going to be me putting one in your ass," Andrew Stone said, stepping out from the side door.

Jim stepped forward next to Andrew, holding a rifle.

John sputtered, "Who cares about that faggot!"

"That's Bull's grandson. He'll own half this ranch one day," Jim growled.

"The fuck he will!" John spat.

"I warned you," Andrew said, cutting off John's tirade. "If you ever abused Maddox again, I'd disown you," Andrew said with a hard look.

His father's tone turned belligerent. "I didn't hit him again! He's a fuckin liar!" John glared at Maddox, fists clenched.

"I said abused. You verbally abused him and threatened to kill River," Andrew said slowly.

"Verbal?" His father spat the word with a sneer. The man didn't comment on the death threat.

"You get off this property. Now," Andrew told his only son. "You're no longer welcome here."

His father raged profanity at them until Jim stepped forward and aimed the rifle at his father's leg.

"You can go walking or limping, it's your choice," the Triple R Foreman drawled.

His father left without another word.

Later that night, they'd gotten the call that John Stone had wrapped his car around a telephone pole. The man had been drunk and died at the scene. Thankfully, the guy hadn't killed anyone but himself.

Andrew offered to call River and tell him about John's death threat but Maddox shook his head.

"I'll see him when he gets home next summer. Just let him be. He's pretty pissed at me."

He'd come home the next summer and every summer thereafter with the hope of rekindling the love he'd pushed away.

Only, River never came back.

Maddox's attention returned to the barn when the mare nudged his back. He gazed blankly around and ran a hand over his face.

Locking up the barn, he slowly made his way toward the house.

CHAPTER TWENTY-TWO

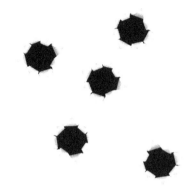

River

MADDOX STONE WAS ONE HARD HEADED, STUBBORN MAN when he believed he was in the right. And for some reason, Maddox thought that keeping the real reason of their breakup a secret was the right thing to do. As if the secret would keep them together. Maddox was so very wrong.

River wasn't giving up. Tracking the man down, River caught Maddox the next morning out on the front porch.

"If you don't talk to me, this is not going to work," he said. Leaning a hip against the railing, he studied the man.

Maddox turned and stared at him, eyes filled with so much emotion it took his breath away.

"There is nothing to talk about," the man said hoarsely.

Anger drew his lips tight, fear that they couldn't get past this made his words come out harsher than intended. "Do you want to make this work?"

"You know I do."

"Then you're going to need to tell me."

"Can't you leave it?"

"No."

"Why? Why can't you leave it alone?"

"I need to know."

"It won't do any good."

"It will for me."

Maddox made an irritated sound in the back of his throat and strode to the end of the porch. River shoved from his lean and went after the man. This was too fucking important to avoid. What they had was too important.

"Maddox, don't walk away from me."

"I'm not, I'm going to get my gear together for the hit on Boyd's place and you should too," Maddox tossed over his shoulder.

"Maddox Stone, you better stop right there if you ever want a chance with me," he hissed.

Maddox stopped and spun slowly. "Did you just give me an ultimatum?"

His heart lurched. "Yes, I did." He tipped his chin up. Fuck it. He was at his wit's ends. "And I wouldn't need to do it if you'd man up and fucking talk to me."

"Man up?" Maddox stalked back to him. "You think that not telling you makes me a wimp?" Maddox asked between his teeth.

"You're the one who called yourself a coward." He threw the man's words back in his face.

The swift sucking of air told him his words had hit their mark.

"River?" Someone shouted from near the pasture. He

didn't turn his head, he only held Maddox's gaze like this was the last chance on earth they had to make things right.

"You're being called," Maddox snarled.

"I don't care," he snapped right back. "We're settling this."

"River!" Oliver called again.

He returned Maddox's glare and snapped at Oliver. "What?" He jerked his head around and found a taxi leaving down the ranch road.

Cris stood not ten feet away from him and Maddox. He sucked in a shocked breath.

Maddox spun as well.

"River?" Cris said hesitantly.

He closed his eyes and let out a slow breath. He opened them and found his gaze held by Maddox's. "Give me a minute, Cris," he called out, not taking his gaze from Maddox.

"You should go," Maddox said tightly, his eyes guarded, his voice filled with anger and hurt. The man tossed a look at Cris and then back to him.

"I didn't invite him here," he hissed.

"But he knows where this place is," Maddox pointed out.

At one time, he'd considered bringing Cris here, but it had been a fleeting moment he'd had during a summer long ago. Summers were the hardest to get through.

"Yes, he knows, but he's not staying."

"Right." Maddox sounded like he didn't believe him.

"Damn it. Stay here. Don't think you're getting out of this."

He waited, but the man said nothing. With a frustrated

sigh, he stalked across the distance and took Cris' arm and drew the impeccably dressed man away from the front steps and back out onto the gravel driveway.

Once he stopped walking, he turned to face Cris.

"Cris," River shook his head. "You shouldn't be here -"

Cris tapped his fingers to his lips, cutting off his words. "I came to tell you that I'm ending it."

"You came to Texas to tell me that?"

"Well yes, I didn't want to end it over the phone." The man's words stung.

"I'm sorry," he said softly, sorrier than he could say for letting them continue for so long.

"It's okay." Cris held his gaze for a long time. "Are you happy, River?"

"I'm trying to be." His throat tightened.

"Then that's what matters, right?" The man leaned in and kissed his cheek.

"You can stay at the house. We can talk more."

"If it's all the same, can you get me a cab? I've got to meet my new man." Cris' smile was brighter than River had seen in a long time.

"I'll have one of the hands drive you to the airport." River offered.

"Thank you."

"Be happy, Cris."

"You too." Cris smiled and turned away.

"I'll take him. I need to get some things in town any-way," Jim said quietly from where the man stood at the railing.

"Thanks, Jim," he said with a last wave to Cris.

He spun, searching for Maddox, and then with a lighter

step, River walked toward where his future stood waiting for him on the porch.

The phone Maddox held against his ear slowed his steps.

The expression on the man's face took his breath away and River suddenly knew without a doubt they were out of time.

∞

Maddox

River's ex-boyfriend stood confident, cool in the heat. The guy was so well put together, not even a strand of hair was out of place. The man was the complete opposite of him. This guy was a bit shorter than him, far skinnier, and wore a cream colored suit...in fucking Texas. The guy's blond hair gleamed in the sunlight and the man's eyes were green. Nothing remarkable, really, he thought jealously.

He pinned his gaze on the pair where they stood at the edge of the drive. Ground his teeth when the blond kissed River on the cheek and smiled. Gave a quick sigh of relief when Jim stepped up and offered the man a ride back to the airport.

His cell phone buzzed and he pulled it out. "Stone," he snapped without even checking.

"Captain Stone."

"Major."

"The informant has surfaced. I need you back here asap. Send me your coordinates, I'll have a chopper pick you up."

His gaze jerked to River as the man walked back to the porch. Their gazes locked and held.

"Understood." He gave his superior his location.

River looked confused and then realization dawned and the man's shoulders suddenly tensed.

Jim walked the ex-boyfriend to the ranch truck, tucked the man inside, and then pulled down the ranch's long driveway. Maddox moved, closing the distance between them.

"I have to go," he said gruffly.

"Yeah," River said flatly. "Of course you do."

"Don't be like that."

"It's a perfect opportunity," River snapped, his look was bitter.

"I have a job to do," he replied, and clenched his jaw.

"You know what? Screw you, Maddox. You had plenty of time to tell me what the fuck happened before you got called back. So kiss my ass," River yelled and spun. Before he could snag River's hand, the man was stalking into the house.

Maddox stood frozen, staring at the empty doorway, his chest aching.

From somewhere inside, River barked out orders.

"Gear up! We're headed to the city. From there, we'll hunt for Rutherford Boyd's assistant."

Shit. He thrust fingers through his own hair on the way back into the house.

He thought he'd have time to find River and say goodbye before he left, but combing the rooms had produced nothing. Suddenly, he was out of time and running for the Black Hawk helicopter that had landed behind the house. He tossed his duffle bag on the bird and jumped in. He sat across from Spencer. He adjusted his head phones and gave the all clear.

The chopper lifted and he glanced toward the ranch. His throat closed when he found River standing in the second story window, with a hand pressed to the glass and Maddox's ability to swallow deserted him. He blinked and lifted a hand to wave.

When River turned away, Maddox closed his eyes.

River wanted the truth. Why couldn't the man let it go and start a future with him?

Would you let it go? a voice in his head said.

He scowled out the open side of the chopper.

"All good?" Spencer asked.

He turned and gave a thumbs up, but his heart was breaking.

Spencer's smirk told him his friend wasn't buying it. He didn't care. He felt too raw.

Why did he fear telling River?

Tell him.

It was too late.

Tell him, he will still love you.

What if he doesn't?

That's a risk you'll have to take. River deserves the truth.

The further away he flew from River, the sicker to his stomach he grew.

"I should have told him," he whispered to himself.

Call him now.

Fumbling for the phone, he sat clenching it in his fist. The chopper was too loud, the call would need to wait. He stared out the open chopper doorway kicking himself in the ass for not telling River in person while he had the chance.

The conversation with himself left him feeling drained

when the helicopter landed at Fort Bliss. The base, located in El Paso, was where they'd receive their orders.

"It's only you and me, buddy. A two-man team," Spencer said as they headed into the building.

He grunted. That didn't surprise him. Sometimes, a two-man team was better. It made getting out of tight places easier. He pushed open the situation room and walked to the laptop at the front.

Spencer followed him inside and shut and locked the door before joining him in the front.

When the laptop powered up, he connected to the video channel and then waited for Major Jones to come on the screen.

"Gentlemen," the man acknowledged them. He went into immediate detail of the informant and the man's location.

"Why'd the informant contact the U.S. instead of Kenya's government?" Spencer asked.

"The man has given us solid intel before and felt safe doing it once again."

"Probably fears for his life." Maddox shared a look with Spencer.

"He's traveled from Somalia to Kenya and is hiding out in a small village. But I don't know of any village in the Boni forest," the major said.

"There aren't any. There's only Kenya military and Somalia insurgents roaming around," Spencer said.

The two countries were still in a maritime dispute and the unrest was high. Somali militants loyal to Al-Shabaab had moved over the border, using Kenya's Boni forest to plan their attacks of terrorism. As a result, Kenya's military was on high alert and had been since the multiple attacks in January.

"Look, it's a simple reach, assess, and escort the informant out and back to the U.S." The major pulled up a map and Maddox leaned forward to split the screen, so both the map and the major's face displayed.

He tapped the coordinates into his tracking device.

"Any questions?" the major asked.

"No, sir," he said and Spencer agreed.

"All right. You can catch a ride on the five AM cargo flight leaving tomorrow morning. They make two outpost stops to unload supplies before landing at the base on the coast. You'll jump sometime after the second outpost and close to the informant's location. I'd prefer if you keep our presence quiet."

Maddox looked at Spencer and the man smirked.

"That's it. I expect you back no later than five days from now."

"Roger that, sir." Eighteen hours to get in, forty eight to get the target, and eighteen or so odd hours to get out. It sounded doable in five days, they might even make it back in four.

"Ground or air extraction?" Spencer asked.

"I'll send a chopper from the outpost to come get you in five days. I'll have them land and pick you up around the same spot you drop in. All you'll need to do is pop smoke. Ground would be your plan B and you'll need to make it to the coast. I don't see you needing the plan B with this operation, gentlemen. Have a good night."

Spencer quirked a brow at him and he smirked. The major made shit sound so easy.

CHAPTER TWENTY-THREE

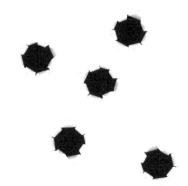

Maddox

SITTING IN THE SEMI-DESERTED MESS HALL WITH SPENCER across from him, Maddox kept mulling over the past.

Spencer was quiet. They hadn't said much and it was his fault. He toyed with a green bean on his fork.

"Okay, spill it," Spencer said.

"Spill what?"

"You're distracted. I don't want you in there with me unless you're at one hundred percent," his partner said bluntly.

He swallowed and carefully set down his fork.

"I let him down."

"What are you talking about?"

"River. I let him down."

"How?"

"We fought because I wouldn't tell him why I ended it between us," he told Spencer.

"Why not tell him?"

He stared at his friend. "I'm going to."

"But why didn't you tell him when you were there?"

"I… I don't want his love to turn into disgust."

"I know about what happened and I'm not disgusted."

"You're the only person I ever told."

"So you love River and you think he'd think less of you?" His friend frowned.

"Maybe." He looked down at his plate.

"You're an idiot. You sound like your old man."

His head jerked up. "Fuck you." He glared, hurt that Spencer would say that.

"I'm not going to sugar coat the truth. Your old man did a fucking number on you. Your years of counseling let you know that. People don't think less of people who've been abused."

He stayed silent.

"If you think so little of him then maybe it's a good thing you walked away and ended it like that."

He glared at Spencer. "His boyfriend showed up! I didn't have a chance," he lied.

"He has a boyfriend?" Spencer looked surprised.

"Well…ex-boyfriend," he muttered.

"Maddox?"

He glanced up.

"You're a fucking idiot."

"Stop saying that!" he growled. "I'm going to tell him."

"Really?" Spencer looked skeptical. "I mean, since you've kept it a secret from him all these years, why tell him now?"

"Because I want a life with him."

Spencer nodded and quirked a smile. "You know exactly what you did by not telling him."

He stared at Spencer for a long time and then closed his eyes. "I took away his choice," he whispered, and opened his eyes.

Spencer's expression was filled with support.

"It's so hard for me to talk about," Maddox whispered.

"Then tell him that when you call him. Tell him why. And say you're sorry," his friend said. "You need to be in the right mindset. Make it happen or I'm pulling us out."

He swallowed. "I was going to pull myself out," he admitted. At least until he knew the outcome of talking to River.

"Make it right, then you won't have to," Spencer said and stood, clamping a hand to his shoulder. Spencer dumped his tray in the trash and then left the mess hall.

He stood and did the same and headed toward the barracks. He found a vacant bunk in a room that wasn't being used and sat on the bed. Pulling out his cell phone, he drew a breath and dialed River's number.

He expected it to go to voicemail and was surprised when River answered only after one ring.

"Seeger," the man clipped into the phone.

"I thought for sure you wouldn't answer," he mumbled.

There was a long moment of silence.

"I almost didn't," River said in a hard, distant voice.

"I'm so sorry," he whispered and reclined on the bed. The silence grew.

"Why?" River asked, the man's tone had changed, going from hard to cautious.

"I'm kicking myself in the ass for not telling you this in person. But when my helicopter took off and I thought that might be the last time I'd ever see you, I knew I had to tell you."

"Tell me what?"

"What I should have told you a long time ago."

"Tell me now."

He took a deep breath, and in slow and halting words, he told River the truth.

"John Stone threatened to kill you if we continued to see each other."

"Do you really think he would have?" River asked after a long moment of silence.

He struggled to get the response out.

"My father threatened to kill my mother when I was a little boy. From my earliest memory, he was always hitting her and choking her. If you ever saw her hospital records, you'd see the proof that he shot at her. The bullet hit the door and splinters went into her face and arm. He told his judge friend that it had been an accident. I couldn't take the chance that he would kill you."

There was a long silence.

"Oh my god, Maddox. He might have tried," River whispered.

"I know." He closed his eyes against the sudden sting. "If you would have stayed and I had gone, he would have tried to kill you."

"You had to send me away." It was a statement, not a question. "I wish you would have trusted me enough to tell me the truth," River said sadly.

"It wasn't about trust, River…That wasn't why I didn't tell you the truth."

"Why didn't you?"

"I was ashamed," he said with a hard swallow.

"Oh, Maddox," River breathed.

"I was so ashamed of what he did to me." The room disappeared in a wash of tears.

"Baby, it was not your fault."

He swallowed and nodded even though River couldn't see him. His breath hitched.

"Oh, Mad," River whispered.

"I didn't want what he did to me touching you in any way."

"You are not your father, you hear me?" River whispered fiercely.

The silence grew while he struggled to regain his control. He rubbed at his nose, swallowed, and grew quiet.

"I wish I was there to hold you." River's loving words washed over him.

"Me too." He wanted River in his arms more than anything in the world.

The silence lingered, but he didn't mind, he could hear River breathing and drew comfort from the sound.

"It's…" he paused and then began again. "It's difficult for me to talk about that time in my life." He wiped at his eyes. "Abuse manifests itself so cunningly, it came out in ways I didn't even realize."

"What do you mean?"

"I didn't realize until talking to Spencer that like my father didn't give me a choice, I wasn't giving you a choice." His voice cracked.

"You were keeping me in the dark," River murmured.

"I know," he whispered. "I'm so sorry."

"I'm glad you told me."

"Me too."

He laid like that, looking up at the ceiling listening to River breathe.

"Now, tell me, who's Spencer? I may need to buy the guy a drink," River's soft voice teased him.

Maddox laughed, wiping at his eyes. "My best friend. You're going to love him."

"If you do, I do. Best friends have a way of making us see sense." River's voice was filled with amusement.

"Oliver?" He guessed River was talking about the guy in his unit.

"Caught that, did you?"

"Yeah, it was easy to see the friendship between the two of you. And I caught the glares more than once," he admitted.

"He's very protective of me."

"I'm glad."

A companionable silence grew and he smiled at nothing, more content than he could ever remember being.

"When do you leave?" River asked.

"In the morning."

"And when you get back?"

"I want to be with you," he said, and then held his breath.

"I want that more than anything in the world," the man whispered.

∞

River

He wanted to hold Maddox tightly. His heart hurt for this man so fucking much and he hated the distance between them.

"I have some leave coming. Beyond the few days I took this week," River murmured.

"Me too. I think I can talk the major into some time off," Maddox said

"Okay then. Do you want to meet at the ranch?"

"No. I want to take you to Aruba," Maddox murmured sexily.

"Aruba?" he laughed softly.

"Yeah, I went there recently and the beaches were white sand, cabanas, the water a color green-blue that you have to see to believe. There's a little resort we can stay at. All the food and drinks you can handle. Laying in the sun and swimming in the ocean." River heard the smile in the man's voice.

"I haven't been to Aruba. I went to Grand Turk once, but not Aruba."

"Then you're in for a treat. I want to reconnect with you, River. I want to hold you in my arms and make love to you again. All day and night if we want." The man's voice held a promise.

"Yes," he breathed. "That's what I want more than anything in this world."

"All right then." Maddox's voice dipped, the deep tone sending a shiver through him. "It's a date. Pick the date for next week and buy tickets." Maddox named a popular resort. "Sometimes, you can get a package deal since it's last minute."

"Next week?" He laughed and rolled onto his back on the bed. "I'll see what I can do. What if I can't get us into the resort next week?"

"Then I'll fly to wherever you are." The man paused. "You weren't living with Cris were you?"

"No. We never got that far. I have an apartment. I'll email you the address."

"I'll be there," Maddox promised.

"River?" Oliver knocked and then poked his head in the door.

"Hang on, Mad," he said and lowered the phone.

Oliver's eyes lifted in surprise.

"Yes?" River smiled.

"We're meeting in thirty minutes to plan the Rutherford raid," Oliver said.

"Okay, I'll be right there," he told the man. Oliver left and he lifted the phone to his ear.

"You heard?"

"Yes. Be careful," Maddox muttered. "I wish I was there to watch your back."

"You'd probably scare away my date and I wouldn't get the keycard," he teased.

"True," Maddox chuckled and then sobered. "Be careful, okay?"

"I will. And Maddox?"

"Yes?"

"You be careful too," he said.

"Always."

CHAPTER TWENTY-FOUR

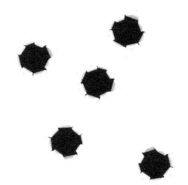

Maddox

SIXTEEN HOURS LATER, THE CARGO PLANE WAS FLYING TOWARD the second outpost tucked away inside Kenya. He and Spencer would air drop this side of the Somalia border.

"It's a cool zone the Kenya military cleared out a few days earlier," the pilot shouted.

He gave the man a thumbs up and traded a short look with Spencer before he jumped out the ass end of the plane.

All he and Spencer had to do was dodge the militant camps, make it to the small village, extract their target, and get to the extraction point.

He pulled his chute cord and braced for the blowback as the harness was jerked along with him upward before floating him back down.

Drifting down into a larger cluster of trees, he hit the ground and rolled. Coming up, he snapped the chute loose, rolled it up in a big wad, and ran to the nearest group of trees. From there, he dropped into a crouch and quickly shoved the chute beneath some shrubs. Lifting his semi-automatic rifle, he took in his surroundings. Spencer had drifted further west than him. He'd give it five minutes and then he'd move.

Lifting a hand, he wiped at the sweat trickling down his face. His shirt grew damp in seconds and clung to his skin in the humid air.

A shuffling came from his right and he slowly eased his rifle toward it. A few seconds later, a bush pig wandered out of the brush, sniffling and snorting and made its way off. The forest grew still save for the sounds of bugs, birds, and the distant trumpet of an elephant. He slowly lifted his radio to his mouth.

"Split Wire, this is Mad Dog, do you copy?" he said, glancing around constantly. The crackling of his radio was all that came back. "Fuck." He grunted and pulled out his jug and took a slow swallow of water to counter the fucking humidity sucking his pores dry. He tucked the jug away and moved.

The Boni forest was an open canopy forest. Between the numerous trees lay large areas of open ground filled with tall, green grass. The grass provided zero overhead cover, but was high enough to duck down and hide from ground enemy.

He moved slowly, weapon at the ready, stopping at each larger tree cluster to pause and listen as he cautiously made his way in the direction he'd last seen Spencer's chute drop.

Gunfire sounded to his left about four hundred yards away, give or take. He spun and ran, taking cover from tree to tree until he reached the perimeter of a small field.

A rusted red jeep sat near the far side of it with two militants taking cover and shooting into the trees. He lifted his binoculars and found Spencer, blood dripping down his forehead, pinned down and returning fire.

He dropped his pack, leveled his M16, and shot a single bullet into one of the men. The other ducked and scrambled around the side of the jeep. Spencer's gun fired and the other man dropped to the dirt.

The area went silent, but he didn't wait, he snatched up his pack and sprung forward, racing across the distance.

"Get the radio!" Spencer yelled.

He stopped at the rusty jeep and found Spencer's radio clipped to the back of one of the enemy's pants and snapped it up and jogged over.

"Can you walk?" he asked, growing closer.

"Yes."

He grabbed up Spencer's pack and kept on running. Spencer broke into a run by his side, but he immediately noticed his friend was favoring his right leg. He kept jogging from tree cluster to tree cluster, trusting that his partner would tell him when to stop. Checking his coordinates, he veered right and kept going until Spencer finally stopped and gasped.

"Need a break."

He spun and slipped his arm around the man's waist and drew him into a small, dense area of the forest. There, he dropped their packs and stood sucking in large quantities of air. He drew out his jug of water and took two swallows before handing it to Spencer. The man took the same number of swallows.

Maddox recapped the jug and then knelt next to Spencer. He gently rolled up the guy's pant leg.

"What happened?"

"My luck, my chute dropped me almost on top of those two."

"Definitely not Kenyan military. None of them were wearing uniforms."

"No, definitely Al-Shabaab militants from over the border." Spencer agreed. "Got that from the landing." The man pointed to the gouge on his right leg.

"And that?" He pointed to the gash on Spencer's head.

"They didn't take kindly to me trying to escape."

Maddox smirked. "Seems like you managed to."

"Yup," his partner drawled.

He pulled out a bandage and wrapped up Spencer's leg tight. The wound wasn't too deep.

The sun sank toward the horizon, sending long shadows of dark over the area. "Let's hunker down." He checked the map. "We're about ten clicks from the informant's location."

They sat side by side against the tree and ate a cold meal.

River

He rapped on the hotel door three doors down and slipped inside when it opened.

"I'm heading down to the bar. I'll text you when I get that key card. I'll hand it off to Oliver and he'll get it back here as planned, make the copy, and then pass it back to me," River said to them.

Oliver followed him out the door. "Everything good?"

He glanced at Oliver. "Yeah, why?"

"You didn't say anything about Maddox calling you."

"That's because I didn't know he was going to call," he laughed.

Oliver quirked a brow.

"Okay. Yes, everything is perfect. He told me what he needed to tell me and we talked it through. We still have some adjustments and further talking, but I think it's going to work. I want it to work," he told his friend, still unable to believe that after all these years, he was officially seeing Maddox Stone again.

"What was the big secret, can you tell?" Oliver leaned a shoulder against the hotel hallway.

River glanced at his watch, he still had twelve minutes to go.

He told his best friend and confidant about the death threat, knowing without a doubt Oliver would never tell another soul. He left out the part of Maddox feeling ashamed or about the abuse, some things were private.

"Holy shit," Oliver gasped.

"Yeah. I mean, I knew that John Stone was scum of the earth, but I never for a moment thought he'd want me dead."

"So, he gave you up to protect you. He must really love you," Oliver said after a long moment.

He smiled at Oliver. "He does."

Oliver grinned and slapped him on the shoulder and River strode on past.

"Hey," Oliver called.

"Yeah?" He spun.

"I like Maddox much better than Cris," Oliver smirked.

"Me too." He smiled. "Be right back." Jogging down the hall, he took the stairs down and entered the restaurant.

It took him a matter of moments to chat the man up and lift the guy's badge. He passed the badge off on his way to the men's room and then returned to the table.

He enjoyed a drink with the assistant while the duplicate was being made. He gave the man a smile and distracted him long enough for Pia to slip the guy's badge back into the man's jacket. When the man turned away to order another round, River lifted the slightly tipsy man's smartphone.

"I'd love another drink, but unfortunately, I need to get going."

"Oh, bummer," the man said. "I thought we could take this to my room."

"Thank you, another time perhaps." He gave the man a smile that was returned before he made his way out of the bar.

Back in his room, he poured himself a drink and changed out of his clothes and into comfortable jeans and t-shirt. A few minutes later, a quiet knock sounded and he opened the door. Pia slipped inside.

"You ready?" he asked.

"Born ready," she grinned, and he gave her the smartphone. She hacked it in minutes and found the address to a warehouse in the downtown district by the train loading docks.

"I'll take Blade and Dillon and do some filming," she said, waving her cell phone.

"I'll drop this back at the bar." He lifted the smartphone. "Text me when you get back and I'll meet you in Elijah's room," he told her.

They met up six hours later when Pia returned from the warehouse with some very interesting film.

The plan was set. The following night, they'd do the hit on Boyd. After they completed the sting on Boyd, the man was going away for a long time.

Hopefully, they'd get this shit done in time for him to be home at the same time as Maddox.

The assistant looked at him with wide eyes but said nothing. Mainly due to the tape sealing the man's mouth shut. The guy wouldn't recognize him due to the black mask completely covering his head except for his mouth and eyes. Just in case, colored contacts took care of turning his eyes from brown to blue.

Holding a finger to his lips, he lifted his gun and moved out of the large entry way and down the hallway.

As planned, Zane and Isaac had entered the building earlier. Rutherford Boyd was working late. The only people left in the building were Boyd, the assistant, and four bodyguards.

Pia, Blade, and Ethan had taken up surveillance points outside.

Oliver, covered from head to foot in black, moved quietly at his side. Elijah was back at the hotel at the makeshift command center Sam had rigged up.

He moved down the hallway and stopped. Oliver

stopped next to him, gun aimed at the hallway behind, covering their flank.

River eased a glance around the corner and found the bodyguards at a table. Three were playing cards and another was in what looked to be a small restroom on the far wall.

He waited until the fourth came out and dropped into the chair and then he stepped out, arms spread wide. He held a gun in each hand, each gun pointed at two suspects.

Oliver did the same, arms outstretched, two guns pointed at the other two guards. The bodyguards gaped in surprise, eyes wide at their silent and sudden entrance.

"No, no," he growled when one reached for the inside of his jacket and the man slowly pulled his hand away. "All right, you two, take out your weapons slowly and put them on the ground."

When all the men complied, River kicked the guns over to a far wall.

Once they had the bodyguards zip-tied and gagged, he moved through the deserted hallway to Boyd's office. He gave Oliver a nod and his friend kicked in the door.

Caught by surprise, Boyd had his pants down. Literally. The man cried out at the intrusion and shoved back from his chair. When Boyd stood, his pants dropped to his ankles. The cries and grunts that came from the laptop on the desk told the story.

"Get dressed," he snapped. Striding to the desk, he slapped the laptop closed.

Boyd struggled to get his pants up and zipped, and then held his hands up.

"What do you want?"

"You." River waved the gun at the guy and motioned toward the door.

Washed out green eyes filled with anger and the man sneered. "I have money."

"Oh, we know that. But you can't buy us. So shut the fuck up," Oliver said before he zip-tied the man's hands behind his back and slapped tape over Boyd's mouth.

River lifted his gun and went back out the way they'd come. Oliver followed with a gun trained on Boyd. River stopped by the break room and checked that the bodyguards were gone, the room back in its pristine order. The assistant's office was the same, the assistant gone and the room in pristine order.

Everything was going according to plan. Stepping out of the back entrance, he loaded Boyd into the van. The bodyguards and assistant were already tucked inside and waiting with the rest of his unit.

Fifteen minutes later, he pulled up to the warehouse district and parked the SUV behind a massive gray building with metal sides and a few missing windows.

Diesel jumped from the passenger side and pulled open the back of the van and waved the gun at the thugs inside. They climbed out one at a time with a few making muffled noises behind the duct tape.

"Keep moving," he said. "You'll all have plenty of time to talk later."

Entering the main room, long tables sat in rows. Each table held stacks of white plastic-covered squares. The drug packages littered the table at one end while the other end hosted buckets and containers of yet to be packaged drugs and paraphernalia. Along one wall sat several workers, hands tied and mouths gagged, courtesy last night of Pia, Blake, and Dillon.

River shoved Boyd down to the floor.

"It looks like your backing up on distribution," he said conversationally. "It doesn't take a genius to see that the missing truck is fucking with your ability to transport drugs."

Rutherford Boyd shouted something behind the tape. River grinned and motioned around the place at Damon Reding's body and the man's dead thugs laying around, their guns near their hands. Zane stepped up and along with Isaac, they dumped the weapons from Boyd's bodyguards on the floor and a few on the table that held the drugs.

"A little rigor mortis has set in and they're starting to smell, but appears to look like a deal gone wrong that ended in shady shit. The big mystery will be how you all got tied up. But I don't think the cops are going to give a shit with all the evidence laying around. Do you?" River asked Boyd.

Boyd's eyes went wide and the man shouted something muffled through the tape and struggled upright until Pia pushed his ass back to the floor. "And stay there," she said, putting the end of her semi-automatic weapon in Boyd's face.

"Gentlemen," River began. "Can I have your attention." He addressed the group and then held Boyd's gaze. Pia walked over and handed him the video she'd taken yesterday.

He stepped up and showed the video to Boyd. The man gave a muffled shout. On the video, Boyd walked next to the tables, testing drugs and talking to the same body-guards and assistant that now sat tied up next to him. One better, Boyd packed white packets of drugs in a suitcase and exchanged money with another man who then left the building.

"Perhaps he's the guy who returned and tied you up," Pia laughed.

"And just so you know," he told Boyd, "this video was taken on a brand new burner phone." River smiled and set the phone in a pile of white powder on one of the long tables. "I'm sure the police will love to see it." He gave a nod and the unit moved in.

The perps were cuffed together sitting back to back in a group on the ground.

Blade made the call to the local detective from another burner phone. Before it went through, she put it on speaker.

"Detective Rice, Narcotics Division," the raspy voice came through the speaker.

The criminals tried making noises behind the duct tape on their mouths.

"I noticed a crime being committed," Blade said, making her voice sound older and shake like a little old lady. She flashed the group of criminals a wide smile. "I was walking Ruffy this morning and I'm positive I saw a crime!"

Zane covered his mouth to stop the chuckle from escaping. River frowned at the guy until Zane moved away, shaking his head.

"What kind of crime, ma'am?" The detective sounded bored.

Blade flashed Zane a wicked smile and continued in a crackling high voice. "It looks like someone tied up drug dealers but left the door to the place wide open. There's drugs everywhere and I'm afraid that somebody is going to come steal them or let those bad men go," Blade said, exaggerating into the phone.

"Yes, ma'am, I will check it out," Detective Rice said, and there was suddenly a sense of urgency in the man's voice.

"Bring backup," she added, ending the call, and laughed. Five minutes later, a distant siren drew close.

"That's our queue." He whirled a finger in the air and the team jogged out to the van. Oliver took the wheel and drove them toward the rear entrance of the warehouse district.

Dillon jumped out and changed the magnetic sign on the side of the van from the electric company to a plumber company. A minute later, they rolled on out of the back gate as the cops came through the front.

A few miles down the road, River took off his black face mask and the others followed suit.

"Too bad we couldn't get him on Triton's kidnapping," Diesel growled.

"I agree," he murmured. "But there was no way of doing that without bringing Gillman and his ranch into the spotlight. The man's been through enough at the hands of Boyd."

CHAPTER TWENTY-FIVE

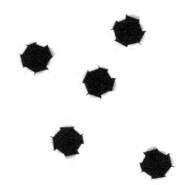

Maddox

H E CROUCHED NEXT TO THE INFORMANT AND REACHED OUT TO
close the man's eyes.

"Looks like they found out he flipped on them,"
Spencer said, checking the area.

"Yeah." Maddox nodded, glancing around at the place
the informant had called a village. It consisted of three falling down huts and a few dug out hiding holes for people.

"He hasn't been dead long. Probably a few hours."
Spencer used his semi-automatic to point at the man.

"I don't like this. Let's get to the extraction site."

"It's going to take us about a day to get there," Spencer
replied.

Maddox glanced toward the sun. That would put them
at the rendezvous spot late the fourth day.

"Better early than being late." He pulled on his pack
and picked up his weapon.

"True," Spencer said, lifting his own bag and wincing when he took step.

"How's the leg?"

"Meh. Only pains me when I walk," the man joked.

He huffed a snort and turned, heading toward a nearby cluster of trees.

Spencer suddenly jerked him to a stop and he went with it, flattening against the trees alongside his partner. He slowly eased his weapon upward and squinted at the tree line ahead.

"At your ten o'clock," Spencer whispered.

He scanned through the scope, his finger tightening on the trigger. "See 'em. We better backtrack."

It looked to be roughly eight militants at a base camp tucked up beneath a large cluster of trees bordering one side of the large, open field they stood at.

Spencer took a step backwards and then another. Maddox did the same. The return trip took them past the dead informant and small huts. Maddox moved on through and kept on going until they were a good quarter of a mile away. From there, they cut around heading to the extraction point by way of the east side.

With the amount of militants occupying the Boni forest, it was getting harder to stay hidden. Spencer stayed strong even with the leg wound. When they were forced to run, the man sprinted like a trooper and only after they dropped back into a walk would he find the man limping.

After backtracking twice more, they stopped when it grew too dark to hike safely.

They took turns on watch and then at first light started out again. They'd reach the extraction point midday if they left now.

A few hours later, they stopped near a copse of trees and gazed at the wide expanse before them. He met Spencer's gaze.

"Let's skirt around it."

Spencer agreed with a tip of his head and headed to the right of the wide open field, staying inside the tree line. Several meters ahead, movement stopped his progress and he put a hand on Spencer's arm.

"What is it?" Spencer whispered.

He pointed and his partner turned his head slowly and spotted another small militant camp. Voices came from their right and he pulled Spencer down.

"Let's belly crawl through the grass," he whispered, nodding to the field of tall grass straight ahead.

Spencer made a sound of agreement and crawled forward. Maddox followed, hoisting his pack and gun on his back. The grass dug into his clothing as he pulled himself through the scratchy blades, using his boots to dig in and propel himself forward. About ten yards in, voices grew closer and he stopped. The voices, suddenly filled with excitement, caused a sour taste of dread to fill his gut.

"They found our tracks." Spencer crawled in earnest.

"Hurry," he urged and picked up the pace. They were half way across the field when voices shouted and drew closer. He grabbed Spencer by the ankle.

"Run!" he told Spencer. His partner popped up and ran. Maddox popped up at the same time, turned, and fired into the group of what looked to be fifteen attackers on their tail. Two men went down and didn't get back up before the rest opened fire. He ducked, fired again, and then sprinted after Spencer, keeping as low as possible.

Bullets peppered the ground and he turned and fired again, causing his assailants to drop into the tall grass.

Spencer, having reached the tree line, returned fire, giving him cover as he continued zigzagging across the open space.

A bullet hit Spencer in the bicep, making a small red mark appear on the man's shirt that quickly widened to a large dark spot.

Spencer jerked and his teeth flashed in a grimace. The man's eyes met his before Spencer brought up his semi-automatic weapon and sent fifty rounds into the group behind him.

Maddox ran, his strides lengthening, as he took advantage of the cover Spencer gave him. Maddox leaped across the distance as another bullet punched a hole in Spencer's lower abdomen.

His friend stumbled back. Across the distance, Spencer's eyes widened with shock and met his. The man's mouth opened in disbelief and hands lifted to press the wound.

"Fuck!" The word tore from his throat as he ran, grabbing Spencer around the waist. He spun Spencer around and sprinted into a run, dragging the man with him.

Bullets cleaved into the trees and bark near his head, sending bits of wood and leaves showering them.

CHAPTER TWENTY-SIX

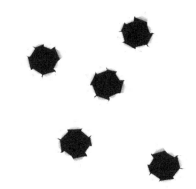

River

FOUR DAYS LATER, AFTER RETURNING FROM THE RANCH AND taking down Rutherford Boyd, the colonel had given the unit some much needed R and R.

He'd made plans to have a drink with Liam and leaving the gym, he headed over to the officers' quarters.

"Hey, Colonel." He grinned at his boss after entering his office. "Ready for that drink?"

Liam said nothing and stared at him. The look in the man's eyes sent his heart lurching.

"River…Come sit down," Liam said quietly.

The world went dim and he vehemently shook his head.

"No."

He backed away. The seat of an office chair hit the back of his legs and he stumbled.

"River…"

"Just fucking tell me!" he hissed, terrified.

His heart pounded in his chest and he couldn't breathe. The duffle bag he held fell from his fingers to the ground with a thud and the sickening taste of fear filled his mouth.

Liam drew in a deep breath and swallowed.

"Captain's Maddox Stone and Spencer Turner went missing in Kenya near the border of Somalia about twelve hours ago," Liam said hoarsely.

He stared at Liam in silence and then reached behind and caught the arms of the chair and his ass hit the seat.

"Tell me everything," he said, his voice so harsh he barely recognized it.

"I was contacted after Maddox and Spencer missed their rendezvous extraction by twelve hours. They went in to retrieve an informant that had possible information about a terrorist group run by Al-Shabaab."

"Who do they report to?"

"Major Gerard Jones."

"Is he sending in a team?"

"No, he believes they're dead."

River stared at Liam, his brain trying to process what the colonel was saying.

"Why were you called?" he asked numbly.

"That's irrelevant," Liam said. "What does matter is I don't think they're dead."

Relief rushed in so fiercely, he felt lightheaded even though the likelihood of them still being alive was slim.

"You're sending me in." It wasn't a question, there was no way in hell he'd stay away.

"Yes. I need you to take in the unit, find them, and

bring them home," the man said, the unsaid *dead or alive* hung in the air.

"Yes, sir." River shoved from his chair and walked to the window. Nothing could keep him away from Kenya. He was bringing Maddox home.

Liam picked up the phone and barked an order to someone. "Find me Captain Elijah Cobalt stat."

Fifteen minutes later, Elijah entered the office and stood at attention. River turned from the view and placed his back to the window.

"Take a seat, Elijah," Liam said.

The colonel's brother slowly lowered into a chair after throwing him a curious look.

"We have a situation, Maddox and Spencer are MIA," Liam said and filled Elijah in on the details.

"Fucking shit," Elijah whispered, staring at Liam.

"You're lead on this mission. I need you to go in with him and bring them home," Liam said, letting out a deep breath.

"Yes, sir." Elijah held his brother's gaze for a long time.

Liam swallowed and then his intense blue gaze pinned both him and Elijah. "Kenyan officials believe you're on a training mission. They do not know about Spencer or Maddox being in the area."

"Excuse me, sir, but how the hell did they get them in without Kenya knowing?" Elijah asked his brother.

"Maddox and Spencer went in dark. They were dropped in by a cargo plane that flies in and out of the area resupplying several outposts and the base further on the coast. It appears that Major Jones didn't inform the base or officials." Liam's eyes were cold and hard.

"Once we get them, what extraction point are we using?"

"The same one Spencer and Maddox had planned. I'll send a Black Hawk. You send me the signal and I'll get that chopper there." The colonel gave them a narrowed look. "I'm not telling you to keep it a secret, but if at all possible, keep Kenya out of this. I'd hate for them to find out one of our own betrayed their trust."

River abruptly nodded. Kenya would take it as an insult that they weren't notified.

"Not a problem," Elijah said.

He blew out a hard breath. He'd accomplished plenty of search and rescue mission like this with one big exception - the person missing in a third world country wasn't the man he loved.

When Liam dismissed them both, River spun, leaving the room with Elijah. Several possibilities played over and over in his head. Maddox was dead, captured, hiding out, wounded, or on the run from terrorists.

"River," Elijah snapped, and he jerked to a stop not looking at the man.

"You okay for this mission, soldier!" his Captain barked.

His head snapped around and he sucked in a quick breath.

"Yes, sir."

"Good, let's get going," Elijah said and sent a text on his phone that swept out to the whole team.

Within fifteen minutes, bodies filled the situation room.

Elijah stood at the front, taking a head count by way of checking off a list clipped to a clipboard.

Pia, Blade, Zane, Diesel, Isaac, Oliver, Dillon, and Ethan were all present. He and Elijah would make it ten.

Not all of them would search for Maddox and Spencer. Some would remain at the base camp as a cover for training. Their best way to keep it secret was to arrive in numbers. Of the ten of them, a few going missing wouldn't bring too much attention. But like Liam said, if he needed to, he'd brave the repercussions and bring Kenya in on what had happened and get their help finding their two lost soldiers.

"Let's move," Elijah ordered.

The team was quiet as they boarded the cargo plane that would fly them to the joint U.S. and Kenya military training base along the African coast.

"Hey," Oliver said quietly, and then sat next to him on the bench-like seat.

He held his friend's gaze. Words were beyond him at this moment.

"We're going to find him," Oliver said.

River nodded and closed his eyes for a brief second. Oliver stayed next to him, not speaking for the duration of the flight.

They landed eighteen and a half hours later at Camp Simba and he and his team were welcomed by the base commander and given bunks among the men and women that made up the Kenya military trainees and base personnel.

Maddox and Spencer had been missing for thirty hours.

In the pitch black of night, they stood around a small table in a command tent provided for their training exercise.

"River?" Elijah said.

He snapped to attention. "Sir."

"You ready?"

"Sir," he said again.

Elijah had hand-picked Isaac and Blade to accompany them on this mission. River's own expertise was in communications and weapons. Elijah wasn't only the unit's commander, but the man served as a medic. Isaac was their operations expert but also skilled with communication. Blade was their weapons expert and currently working to qualify as a medic.

The four of them left the camp beneath the cover of darkness. He set up a grueling pace. They located the drop zone and Blade found one of the parachutes Maddox or Spencer had used. They located another chute further away from the first and tucked behind some trees.

Night vision goggles helped them avoid Somali militants and Kenyan military. It was a good thing because at this point, River would put a fucking bullet in anyone who got in his way.

He wasn't running. They weren't supposed to be seen, engage in firefights, or get caught, but he wasn't running from a fucking terrorist.

Elijah located shell casings that suggested either Maddox or Spencer or both had been shot at. The rusted jeep stood in a small field and next to it lay two dead men.

"Military grade weapons like the ones Maddox or Spencer carry killed these guys," Isaac said.

"Good boys," River murmured.

"They're deadly," Blade said, quietly taking in the carnage. "They fucked these guys up."

"Let's hope they stayed that way," he said.

They moved on, searching and tracking to the site that

supposedly housed the informant. The man was dead and had been for a day and a half if the flies coming from his wound and eyes and the smell were any indication.

After a moment of checking the area, they moved on. They came upon a deserted militant camp that was probably two days old.

"River, look." Isaac spotted a flattened area near the edge of the field that suggested an encounter had happened there.

"Over here too," River said, and followed the path through the waist high grass and found a spot with shell casings, fifty or more, and signs of blood.

"They took off that way." Blade stood and pointed. "Looks like one is wounded."

He nodded and they eased through the night. Each step carefully placed.

CHAPTER TWENTY-SEVEN

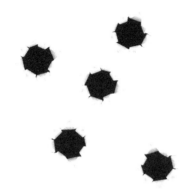

Maddox

"A HHHHH," HE SCREAMED THROUGH HIS CLENCHED teeth and then spat in the militant's face.

The guy backhanded him and the crudely fashioned chair toppled back. His head hit the ground, but at least the punches to his body had stopped for the moment.

The crack to the head wasn't enough to take him out. Someone shouted in Somali and another gave an order. He was cut from the chair and lifted. He sagged his whole weight down as if he were passed out, making them drag him to the crudely made prison. The thatch-like door was unlocked and he was tossed inside.

He slammed onto the ground, pain glancing through his shoulder and into his ribcage, and he rolled to his side, biting back a gasp. Then the door was shut and a chain wrapped around with a padlock. Two guards stood outside the door.

He closed his eyes and drew in shallow breaths, trying to regulate his breathing. He wiped at the sting of blood and sweat that dripped into his eyes and grimaced. It took several minutes of lying there and several more struggling before he pulled himself to one of the walls. Once there, he sat with his back against it, resting for a moment.

Carefully, he moved a pile of leaves away from a small area next to him and began scooping out the dirt. The hole was growing, he only hoped he'd last until he could get it big enough to get out.

He leaned sideways and looked through the thick wood slats toward another hut. His vision was blurred and it took him a while to focus. One eye was completely swollen shut and he couldn't breathe out of his nose and he suspected his jaw might be cracked, but he was finally able to focus with one eye closed and the other open.

A chain on the door of the other hut held it shut. A lump grew in his throat. Spencer had stopped screaming sometime early last night. Their captors had stopped entering the other structure. He blinked, closing his eye at what that might indicate.

Over the next few minutes, he carefully scooped the dirt out of the small hole, careful not to make his fingers raw. Raw skin would give him away. He must have passed out, because a shout and scuffle outside jerked him awake. He quickly placed the leaves back over the hole.

Gunfire from a suppressed M16 filled the night. The fuckers were at it again, shooting his and Spencer's semi-automatic weapons into the trees. They'd been doing that the past day and laughing. Maybe he'd get lucky and the sons of bitches would shoot themselves.

Covering the hole wore him out and he sat gasping in short, sharp bursts. He poked his tongue at his cracked and swollen lips. Trying to swallow was like trying to chew rock and sand. Thirst was making it hard to focus.

The door and chain rattled and every muscle in his body went tight. Scooting as far as he could, he settled into stillness and waited.

They were coming for him sooner than anticipated. Usually, they let him be for a few hours between beatings. He slowed his breathing and closed his eyes. He probably wouldn't last much longer. Sometime last night, when Spencer stopped screaming, he'd realized they probably weren't going to make it out alive.

A scuffle and soft gurgle and a thud sounded and he blinked open his good eye. Rolling, he made it to his hands and knees. Had they gone after Spencer again? He lifted up, resting on one knee, and shoved upright. Swaying, he used the side of the enclosure for balance. The chain around the door gave way as if someone cut it and then the door was yanked open.

Blinking, he held up a hand to block the light from blinding him.

"Maddox," River whispered.

At least he thought it was River, but then he'd been hallucinating about the man for the past forty or so hours.

He made a noise deep in his throat, not words, but more like an *"I'll kill you fuckers"* sound and dared them to come closer. He curled his hands into fists and swayed with pain splintering his skull and thirst clawing at his throat.

"Shhh. It's okay," the voice tricking him said and came closer.

He jerked back and bumped against the wall and lifted his hands in a fighting position.

The man holding the flashlight turned it on himself and the most beautiful sight on earth appeared.

"River?" he croaked.

River moved then, drawing closer.

"Sorry I'm late." River offered a wobbling smile.

"You were cutting it close, Seeger," Maddox mumbled the grateful words back and then eagerly put his lips to the jug of water River held to his lips.

"I won't let it happen again," River vowed fiercely.

Guzzling, water poured down the front of him as he tried to take it all at once. River let him have his fill and he eventually stopped and let the jug go. River capped it and then slipped an arm around his waist.

Cracking his one good eye further open, Maddox pulled River to him and buried his bloodied face into the man's neck and held on. River squeezed him gently, thankfully, because Maddox thought his ribs might be broken.

Why was Infinity here? Why not his own unit? He took a step and winced but River didn't let go and guided him outside. Isaac and Blade stood waiting. A sea of enemy bodies lay scattered around the camp.

"Jesus, Maddox. I hope you got some payback," Isaac said.

"You bet I fucking did," he rasped, thinking of the militants he and Spencer had gunned down before they were captured.

"Hello, Maddox," Blade said and smiled at him.

"Hello, Blade," he whispered, and then River was helping him walk away from the camp.

"Wait…" he rasped and stopped walking.

River glanced up at him.

"Spencer…"

River took in a breath and closed his eyes for a brief second. When he opened them, pain swirled in their brown depths.

"I'm so sorry, Maddox."

The camp became quiet. The only sound that of a slight breeze, the low hum of insects, and the sharp cry of a wild animal.

The tears came hot and hard as he struggled to cope. River's arm tightened around him. Sucking in several breaths, he tried to contain his noise but it bubbled up. River held him and he buried his face in the man's neck, clutching at River tightly as a knife carved a hole out of his heart.

He drew back and took a shaky breath.

"River?" A large figure came from the hut next door and stood in the doorway.

"Yes?" River turned to Elijah, keeping a tight arm around his waist.

"I've got a faint pulse." The large man stooped and hurried back into the hut.

He jerked away from River and stumbled to the hut and ducked inside. River was at his back when he entered. He moved to Spencer and dropped down beside the man. Lowering his head to Spencer's chest, he heard the faint heartbeat.

"I thought he passed away." River frowned at Elijah in confusion.

"He did, but I was able to get his heart going again," the man said quietly.

"Thank you," Maddox told Elijah, and the man nodded.

"He's lost a lot of blood. It looks like they stopped beating on him and tried to patch him up to keep him alive longer." Elijah took several minutes to slip a needle into Spencer's arm, set up an IV drip, and then he placed the fluid bag on Spencer's chest. From there, Elijah stood and stepped up to Maddox and looked him over.

"I'm okay." The words came out roughly through his tight throat.

Elijah nodded and flashed a light in his one good eye and then over his face and down his chest. He was shirtless. "I'll wrap those," the man said and he stood still without arguing. Elijah quickly wrapped his ribs and he had to admit it helped. Then the man stepped back and hurried back to check on Spencer.

Turning slowly, he found River standing close.

"Thank fuck you're here." He didn't know how nor why River had come to find him and Spencer, but he was more grateful than he'd ever been in his life.

"Always," the man murmured the last word he'd spoken during their last conversation.

River held out a shirt and helped him slip it on before handing him the water jug. He took several more grateful swallows before handing it back. He placed a hand on River's back for balance as the man helped him pull on a pair of socks and boots.

"We need to walk out of here," River ordered, holding his gaze.

He gave a slow nod because anything else killed his head.

Blade unrolled and snapped out a burlap heavy duty tarp in the shape of a bed roll and attached a harness.

Isaac moved in with two long pieces of wood and attached them to the underside of the tarp.

Elijah carefully lifted an unconscious Spencer and placed him on the crudely fashioned sled and then strapped him and the IV bag into place. Once Spencer was secure, Elijah picked up the harness and put it over his own head. The large man adjusted it over his shoulders and around his chest.

River handed Maddox a semi-automatic M16 and held his gaze. "I know you're having trouble with your vision. Just don't shoot me." The sexy man gave a half smile.

He huffed a laugh that sounded more like a grunt. "I'll do my best."

CHAPTER TWENTY-EIGHT

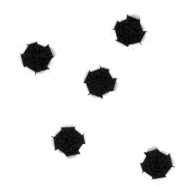

River

B LADE JOGGED UP TO HIM FROM THE REAR. "HEY, RIVER. WE should probably find shelter."

She was right. Dawn was starting to break over the horizon. "Okay, let's look for a place."

Elijah agreed and they located a spot beneath a heavily wooded cluster of trees and shrubs. Rations and water were distributed to all but Spencer. Elijah changed the man's IV bag and gave both Spencer and Maddox a shot of penicillin to help ward off infection.

"We're not going to base camp, are we," Maddox said softly from his side.

"No." He glanced up from his food and held the man's gaze. "We're heading to the original extraction site that you two were supposed to rendezvous at."

"Is that the closest way out? I don't know exactly how far me and Spence had been taken," Maddox admitted.

"It is the closest, yes. The camp we found you at wasn't too far." He showed Maddox the coordinates and gave the man a half smile. "You'll be home before you know it."

"And you?"

He studied the man's swollen and bruised face and lifted a hand to cup the side of Maddox's neck. He squeezed gently. "I'll go back to base camp, collect the unit, and then I'll be home."

"Thank you, River. Fuck...thank you." The sincerity that broke Maddox's voice was almost his undoing.

"You had to know I'd come for you," he said over a suddenly tight throat. His eyes burned into Maddox's.

"I thought...I'd hoped." Maddox cleared his throat and nodded.

"I'd like to think you'd do the same for me," he admitted.

"Without hesitation," the man whispered and swallowed, reaching for him. They held each other, tucked in the safety of camouflage and trees. Maddox buried his face against his neck and River tightened his arms.

"I love you," Maddox whispered.

River drew back, searching Maddox's gaze with a smile. "I've waited forever to hear those words from you again."

"I never stopped loving you," Maddox admitted.

"You must know how much I love you."

"Oh yes, baby," Maddox whispered. "I have no doubts."

He leaned back against the tree and patted his lap. Maddox slowly adjusted until he was stretched out on the ground and placed his head on his lap. River adjusted the camouflage branches and glanced around in the growing morning light. He gazed down at his love and combed his fingers through Maddox's hair until the man's good eye drifted closed.

He swiveled his head slowly until he found Blade on watch. He wouldn't have been able to see her if he didn't already know where she was. Looking like an extension of a cluster of trees, Blade gave him a thumbs up that he returned with a faint smile.

Elijah sat a few feet from Spencer. The pair were completely covered by a large camouflaged netting. The captain held a semi-automatic weapon at the ready. The man constantly combed the area.

Isaac was laying in the tall grass about five yards from them completely camouflaged with branches and grass keeping a watch on the area.

The heat and humidity had him drenched, but he held still as much as possible while Maddox slept.

As soon as night swept over the forest, it became time to move. He gently stroked his fingers through Maddox's hair to wake the man. Maddox didn't jerk awake, but rather a small crease etched between the man's dark brows and then this time, both lids flickered open, revealing bright blue eyes.

Maddox gave him a slow, crooked smile that River returned before he stood and carefully helped the soldier to his feet. They relieved themselves and then hydrated. While Maddox was cleaning up with a wet rag and eating down some of the rations, Elijah filled River in on Spencer's condition.

"He's not doing too well. We need to get him out of here soon," Elijah said.

"Okay. If we hit it hard tonight, we should be able to reach the extraction site before dawn."

"Agreed," Elijah said and adjusted the harness over his shoulders.

He took up the lead keeping Maddox beside him. If they didn't reach the extraction site by dawn, then they'd have to chance walking in the daylight because he doubted Spencer was going to make it another night.

The way was slow going. Maddox stumbled and wobbled and he slipped one arm around the man's waist and held his weapon in one hand pointed forward.

"Sorry," Maddox mumbled.

"It's okay." River kept his pace strong. Everything in him wanted to slow down, but he couldn't risk it. They were going slow enough by pulling Spencer on the makeshift sled. Elijah took the brunt of it with his size, but every once in a while, the man let him and Isaac take over the reins. Usually, after being guilted into doing so. Elijah seemed to make it his sole mission to get Spencer to the site without help.

"Possible Somali militants fifty yards ahead to the right," Isaac's whisper came through the small device he had tucked in his ear.

"Roger. Isaac come help me unharness. Blade flank us," Elijah ordered. River lowered Maddox against a tree. They pulled Spencer in the sled as close to Maddox as possible. He held his lover's gaze in the darkness. He handed Maddox his weapon once the man eased to the ground, his back to a tree.

Once settled, Maddox held the gun across his thighs, placed his free hand on Spencer, and gazed up at him.

Isaac crouched next to Maddox and Spencer, the man was their last line of defense should the enemy punch through.

"Stay here. I'll be right back," he said quietly.

"You better." Maddox's voice held a fierceness that drew a slight smile from him.

"You can count on it," he whispered, and then slipped through the darkness. Not letting the enemy get any closer to their wounded, he skirted around to flank them.

Isaac was correct. It was militants in a group of four heading their way.

He stilled near a tree cluster and a few feet away from him, Blade sank into the waist high grass. Elijah had already disappeared out there somewhere.

Voices drew near, the soft murmur of Somali, the crunch of boots on grass and wood and in the next second, they were next to him.

He lunged out, slammed his gun against the nearest man, and knocked the guy backwards. Sprawled, the militant lifted his gun but River kicked it aside. The weapon discharged and sent several shots firing into the darkness.

Damn it! He slammed the butt of his weapon into the man's throat, crushing his windpipe. Blade swooped up from the grass and sent a knife into the second perp's spine, then sliced the man's throat from behind. Elijah came up out of the darkness and shot twice. Each soft snick, snick of the man's silencer sent bullets into the two remaining enemies, taking them out of action permanently.

"We need to hurry. Someone may have heard the shots."

They hustled back, collected their wounded, and moved quickly. Three hours later, they drew near to the extraction site. He slowed and lifted his hand, the team behind him stopping completely. The small field sat a few yards ahead of them.

"That's it," Maddox whispered.

He nodded and lowered Maddox against a nearby tree. Elijah pulled Spencer closer to Maddox and then unharnessed himself. He, Blade, and Elijah fanned out a few yards to check for hostiles.

"Clear," Elijah murmured.

"Me too," River returned.

"Same," Blade said and Isaac echoed.

Pulling off his pack, he took out the radio and sent the message to the colonel. The coded message came back that help was on the way and to sit tight.

They hunkered down. The air felt tense. The Black Hawk arrived forty five long minutes later.

The chopper came in hot and hard. When the bird landed, the rest of Infinity jumped out. They surrounded him and their wounded.

It was one of the hardest things he'd ever done letting Maddox get on the chopper without him, but he had a job to do.

He gripped Maddox tightly around the shoulders, careful of his ribs, and then helped him into the helicopter. He caught the man's hand.

"If you need a place to recuperate," he yelled over the noise. "Show the email I sent you with my address on it to Colonel Cobalt and he'll give you the spare key."

Maddox's lips tipped and the smile reached his eyes.

River turned and ran stooped over until he was out of range of the deadly blades and with the rest of his unit. Then he turned to look back.

The Black Hawk lifted off, but he held Maddox's stare until the man was lost to view.

CHAPTER TWENTY-NINE

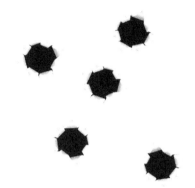

Maddox

"**A**H SHIT," HE HISSED BENEATH HIS BREATH WHEN HE TWISTED in the helicopter seat.

It had taken roughly twenty-five hours to get back on U.S. soil. They'd stopped briefly at a makeshift hospital. The doctor shook her head. Spencer had internal damage from the bullet in his abdomen and his chances were grim. She had stabilized Spencer as much as possible before they boarded the cargo plane back to the US. A Black Hawk helicopter stood waiting to fly them into Infinity's base.

Four soldiers ran forward and one stepped up to give him a hand. He let the guy help him out and then stood as they unloaded Spencer before walking next to the gurney.

"Let's get you squared away," one of the men said.

"Thank you."

"Colonel Cobalt is waiting." One soldier pointed, drawing his gaze.

A large figure stepped out from the hanger and long strides brought the man near.

"It's good to see you safe, Captain Stone," the colonel said and shook his hand.

"Thank you, Colonel, thank you for sending Infinity for us." He gripped the man's hand hard.

"You're welcome," Liam said, and then turned from him. The man's eyes were glued on Spencer. The colonel stepped closer and put his hand on Spencer's shoulder.

Maddox watched curiously. Liam closed his eyes and took a deep breath before he stepped back and the men stepped forward to lift Spencer into the waiting ambulance.

"I've arranged for you to have a ride home," the colonel said.

"Home?"

"To the ranch?" The man frowned.

"I have a better idea." He showed the man the email from River.

"All right. That's doable, but first you get checked out," the colonel ordered. "Then report to my office."

"Yes, sir."

River's apartment was quiet and had a view of the lake. It wasn't big, but it was really quite perfect. It was a place Maddox could definitely relax. He pulled out his phone and ordered food through the app and then slid open the patio door.

Stepping out onto the small balcony, he gingerly lowered into one of the soft chairs. He closed his eyes beneath the warmth of the sun and drifted to the sounds of birds squawking near the shore, cars in the distance, and people talking somewhere.

It had been a week since his return and he still hadn't heard a word from River. Liam assured him the man was safe and taking care of some additional training excursions in Kenya.

The doorbell rang and he struggled to his feet with a wince. Tugging open the door, he thanked the guy for the food and headed back to the patio. He sat the containers on the small foot stool nearby and ate bent over the boxes. Slurping up noodles and sweet covered chicken, he savored the taste.

He finished the food and chugged down some water. Easing back into the chair, he went back over the conversation he'd had with his own commanding officer while in the hospital.

"Welcome back, Captain Stone," Major Jones said from his hospital bedside.

When he'd gone to get checked out as ordered by Colonel Cobalt, Maddox had been admitted for overnight observation.

He had agreed because they had to do an MRI and CAT scan on his ribs and head. The ribs were broken and his nose was fractured, along with a hairline crack in his lower jaw bone. His nose had been reset, his ribs taped, and the jaw would heal slowly on its own if no more blunt force trauma interrupted the healing.

He gave the major a flat stare.

"I'm putting in for a transfer," Maddox said, narrowing his eyes on his commander.

"Understandable." Jones looked uncomfortable. *"Let me know where and I'll make it happen."*

For some reason, and maybe because he was pissed off at the guy, those words felt like an admission of guilt. Had the major really planned on leaving them there without knowing if they were dead or alive?

"I suspect that Spencer will be transferring as well," he said.

"He's already voiced his request," the man admitted.

Maddox gave the major one of what he hoped to be his last salutes. He'd been released the next day and he'd stopped by the hospital computer room. Taking over one of the computers, he filled out the necessary paperwork for the transfer. Hopefully, it would come through before he was cleared from medical leave.

A train whistle in the far distance snapped him out of his thoughts and back to the peaceful balcony. Too tired to stay awake any longer, he gathered the trash and tossed it away before turning toward River's bedroom.

From the first moment he'd seen it, he'd loved it. The bed was huge, king sized, with a warm, brown comforter. It had drawn him immediately. He turned to the right and headed down the short hallway into the bathroom that held a large shower. Once clean, he crawled beneath the covers and sank into the softness and slept.

Sometime later, the bed dipped and jerked him slightly awake.

"It's only me," River whispered, and then slipped beneath the sheets.

The man was naked and smelled like soap and he groaned, pulling River into his arms. His own briefs felt restrictive until River smoothed them down his hips, along his legs, and pulled them off before slipping back up his body. Their skin brushed and River caressed his cock and he moaned, arching beneath the man's touch.

"River," he breathed. The searching and stroking touch of River's palms as they gently skirted his ribs and brushed over his abs, then nipples in slow, circular movements drew his hips from the bed. The man's mouth traced along his hip bone and then his wet, hot tongue slowly licked at the slit along his crown.

"Yes," he moaned and then River took his cock into his mouth and kept going until the head nudged deep at the back of his throat. It was hot and wet and he helplessly undulated beneath River's mouth.

Maddox thought he'd explode with the pleasure from the wet heat coating his dick as River sucked harder. The mouth around him felt like a tight, wet fist as it slipped slowly up and down. River swept his tongue along the vein beneath his dick, pressing hard until his balls drew up. He wanted to call out, but he couldn't. He could only groan until he spasmed and convulsed, pumping his cum into the man's waiting mouth.

$$\infty$$

River

He groaned around the convulsing cock and drank down every bit of Maddox's release until he grew limp. Then River lifted up to rest his head on the man's hip, careful of his ribs.

"Come here," Maddox whispered, and he lifted upward and carefully arranged himself at the man's side, his head on Maddox's shoulder. "Get the lube."

The order drew a smile and he reached and opened the

small drawer by the bed. Grabbing the bottle of lube, he tipped his head back.

"You can't have sex." He held Maddox's glittering gaze.

"Who says?"

"I do, and probably the doctor."

The man's lips pursed in a semi pout. "I have another idea."

Maddox dumped lube into his palm and then reached down between River's legs.

"Oh fuck," River said when the man's slicked up hand closed around his hard cock. "Yes," he hissed and thrust into Maddox's closed fist.

"That's it, fuck my hand," Maddox urged, picking up the pace.

River lifted his head and kissed the man's lips. Tongues laved, teeth nipped, and he flicked his own nipples while Maddox worked him with a quick and twisting grip.

"This is what I want you to do to my ass when I'm better," Maddox whispered hotly into his mouth. The vision sent him into overdrive. Hips snapping wildly, his release carved into his balls and cock, slammed into his gut, and he exploded in the hand that held him. River gasped into Maddox's mouth, sucking at his tongue wildly and thrusting until he was spent and lay gasping.

He rolled and pinched several tissues from the box on the night stand and cleaned up the mess and wiped Maddox's hand before he tucked in close beneath the covers.

"It was nice coming home knowing you were here."

"I like it here." Maddox hugged him close. "Especially now that you're here. And, your balcony is killer."

"Right? It's one of the reasons I took the place."

"I can see why."

He ran his hand over Maddox's chest and dropped into silence for a moment.

"How's Spencer?" He gazed up into the man's blue eyes.

"It's slow, but he's recovering," Maddox said.

"Good."

"You should have seen the colonel's face when we got off that chopper."

He lifted up curiously. "What do you mean?"

"That man was beside himself over Spencer being hurt."

"I think Liam's been keeping tabs on Spencer."

"Wait," Maddox said. "Back up."

River grinned. "The colonel said that Major Jones wasn't going in to get you guys. I asked Liam how he knew that you were even missing."

"How did he know?" Maddox frowned.

"The only way he could have known was if he was keeping an eye on Spencer. He could find him at any given time."

"True. But there's another logical explanation."

"What?"

"If he's listed as Spencer's emergency contact," Maddox said.

His mouth gaped. "You think?"

"Maybe, I don't know."

"Well, whatever the reason, I'm glad the colonel found out you were missing."

"Me too." Maddox smiled and pulled him close.

EPILOGUE

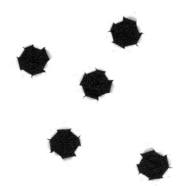

River

Three months later

LIAM EYED THEM FROM ACROSS HIS DESK. "SO, YOU WANT TO JOIN Infinity, Captain Stone?"

"Yes, sir," his lover said.

"Why should I do that?" Liam tapped his chin.

"Because he's one of the best and you could use that on this team," River growled, affronted that Liam would stall.

"I have the best," Liam pointed out, giving him a hard stare.

"I won't beg," Maddox rumbled, and Liam flipped his gaze from him to Maddox.

River squinted at his boss. "You either gain one or you lose one."

Liam suddenly huffed with a chuckle. "I reached in and pulled Maddox's application for transfer the minute it was submitted. You asking me to join is unnecessary. I was set to offer as soon as you were cleared."

"You can do that?" River teased his boss.

Liam's grin widened. "Yes, I can."

Maddox chuckled.

Liam stood and shook Maddox's hand. "Welcome to Infinity, Captain."

"Thank you, Colonel."

"What about Spencer?" Maddox asked.

"Your friend is pissed at me," Liam sighed.

River's curiosity notched up hard, but before he could say anything, Maddox was speaking.

"He'll get over it, just offer him a job." Maddox frowned.

"I have," Liam said, and then looked away. "I don't think he'll take it."

"That's too bad," River said, but he couldn't be too sad, because Maddox was in his unit. When they next went into battle, they'd have each other's backs. It was a win-win to him.

The past several months had been an adjustment period. They'd stayed at the apartment until Maddox was cleared to fly. Then they'd flown back to Texas and shared the news with Bull and Triton, who were thrilled for them. They'd purchased tickets to Aruba and spent four days in the sun. They'd had such a good time, they were planning another trip next year.

Life was odd, he mused. In a way, Maddox sending him away or rather ending it had unknowingly put him on the path to a career he loved. He would have never joined the Army and gone into Special Forces if Maddox hadn't broken up with him all those years ago.

While he was sad at the eight years apart, he thanked whatever powers that had brought them back together even if it had been his grandfather's unplanned adventure into drugs.

He'd had a stern talking to Bull about that and was assured nothing like it would ever happen again. Gillman wiped Bull's debt clean and made a friend for life.

As for the ranch, they'd pooled their resources together and brought the ranch back into the green. Triton was still adjusting after the kidnapping. The young man said he couldn't be in the dark any longer. River tried talking to Triton about seeing a counselor, but the boy dodged him. Maddox said to give it time, so he'd backed off.

As for his man, his lover had healed nicely, although his nose remained a tiny bit crooked. They'd discussed moving in together and were making plans to see one of the larger apartments in the same building, preferably with a balcony. Life was going better than he ever dreamed possible with Maddox at his side.

"Meeting in ten minutes," the colonel said and stood. "Walk with me, gentlemen."

They headed down together to the meeting room. He took a seat near the front and Maddox took the one next to him.

The team entered and more than a few of them threw curious looks their way.

"So…you got Maddox attached to your hip I see, huh?" Oliver said cheekily.

"Grow up." He rolled his eyes.

The unit chuckled. Maddox grinned. "I'll stay attached to his…ahem … hip anytime."

"Oh!" Isaac cackled loudly. "Gotcha, Olive!"

"It's Oliver, I...ass...ic," Oliver razed the man back. Isaac danced around the guy, throwing mock punches.

"Kids," Diesel grumbled when Oliver bumped into him and almost spilt the giant's coffee.

"Oops," Oliver laughed and avoided Isaac by keeping Diesel between them.

Blade stuck her leg out and Isaac tripped right into Zane, who caught him.

"Knock it off or you're gonna get hurt," Zane growled and sent Isaac away.

"If you're all done horsing around, I can use your attention up here," Liam called from the front of the room.

Everyone standing took a seat and gave their leader their complete attention.

"Captain Maddox Stone is Infinity's newest member. I have made an offer to Captain Spencer Turner, but I haven't heard back yet."

"What's asshat Major Jones have to say about it all?" Zane said unwisely.

"That's enough." Liam pinned Zane with a hard look. "Neither you nor I may have agreed with Major Jones' decisions, but he is still an officer and your superior."

"Sorry, sir." Zane looked down at his hands.

"Apology excepted," Liam said. "Now, first order of business."

The voices in the room faded beneath the heated look Maddox gave him. Their eyes met and his heart picked up its silly beat of love. It wouldn't always be easy, but he'd spend the rest of his days on earth forging out a life with this man by his side.

∞

Maddox

He leaned against the balcony railing and sipped at the cup of coffee he held. They had a short reprieve, three days, and then he'd be going on his first mission since joining Infinity. Never in his wildest dreams would he have ever pictured him and River going on a mission together. He hadn't felt this level of excitement for the job in a long time. He smiled and took another swallow of the hot brew.

Joining Infinity had been a no brainer. He suspected that Colonel Cobalt would pick him up when he put in the transfer and he hadn't been wrong.

River hadn't needed to go marching into the man's office, but it was cute the way River had stood up for him. River's *"he's in or I go"* attitude warmed his heart. What he hadn't expected was Spencer's anger.

"Why'd you go and join Infinity?" Spencer growled.

"I need to be where he is. Can't you understand that?"

"I guess," Spencer sighed, and plucked at the hospital bed sheet.

"I love him, Spence."

"I know," his friend admitted after a minute. "Sorry I got mad."

"You can come too. The colonel wants you," he told his friend, and carefully observed the man's expression go blank every time he mentioned Colonel Liam Cobalt.

"Infinity is no place for me," Spencer hedged.

"I think you're wrong."

"Anyway," the man said after a moment, *"I'm happy for you."*

River stepped out onto the balcony and joined him at the railing, effectively bringing his attention to the here and now.

He turned and slipped his arm around the man's shoulder and drew him close.

"Hey, love."

"Hey."

River smiled up at him and he couldn't resist lowering his head for a kiss. After a long moment, he drew back and smiled, loving the way the gold flecks of the man's eyes glittered in the sunlight.

"The guys are getting together for a game of poker and pizza tonight. Wanna go?" River asked.

"Yeah, that sounds like fun."

"It does, doesn't it?"

"As long as I get to be with you, I don't care where I am," he said, sounding corny, but he suspected River loved it by the look on the man's face. And keeping River happy had become his main goal in life.

He'd truly found home in River's arms.

The end

AUTHOR'S NOTE

Thank you for reading *Cutting it Close*. Stay tuned for more stories about alpha men who protect their own. Please feel free to leave a review, we authors' love that! You can reach me on Facebook, Twitter, and Instagram. My email address is Reeseknightleyauthor@gmail.com

ACKNOWLEDGEMENTS

To my fans, as always, these stories are for you.

ABOUT THE AUTHOR

Reese spends her time creating stories from the characters rattling around in her head. Her love of reading mystery, action and adventure, and fantasy books led to her love of writing. Reese works as a full-time writer. She loves to hear from her readers.

OTHER BOOKS BY REESE

Out for Justice Series

Ricochet

Collide

Rampage

Destruction

Made in the USA
Las Vegas, NV
28 February 2021